Henri L

SISTER SPLIT

SISTER SPLIT

BY

SALLY WARNER

American Girl®

CHILDRENS ROOM

Published by Pleasant Company Publications
Text Copyright © 2001 by Sally Warner
Cover Illustration Copyright © 2001 by Sue Clarke

Visit our Web site at **americangirl.com**

Printed in the United States of America.
First Edition
01 02 03 04 05 06 RRD 10 9 8 7 6 5 4 3 2 1

The characters and events portrayed in this book are fictitious.
Any similarity to real persons, living or dead, is coincidental
and not intended by the author.

AG Fiction™ and the American Girl logo are trademarks of Pleasant Company.

Library of Congress Cataloging-in-Publication Data
Warner, Sally.
Sister split / by Sally Warner.—1st ed.
p. cm. "AG fiction."
Summary: When her parents separate, eleven-year-old Ivy must cope not only
with their impending divorce but also with the unexpected impact it has on
her relationship with her older sister.
ISBN 1-58485-372-7 (pbk) ISBN 1-58485-373-5 (hc)
[1. Sisters—Fiction. 2. Divorce—Fiction. 3. Family life—Fiction.] I. Title.
PZ7.w24644 Si 2001 [Fic]—dc21 2001023970

To my sister, Susan Todd Jackson,
and to happy endings

1

CONTENTS

1
PAY THE TOLL

"I HATED IT WHEN YOU WERE BORN," MY SISTER tells me right before she switches off her reading light.

And we haven't even been fighting or anything. I was half asleep, in fact.

She's probably just mad because she had to stay home with me this afternoon while Mom took Mrs. Pincus, our neighbor, to the supermarket.

Not that I really need a baby-sitter—I'm almost twelve. Lots of girls my age *are* baby-sitters. But I don't mind it when Lacey stays with me. To tell the truth, I kind of like it, because when I'm home alone, I'm always thinking doorknobs are turning or the stairs are creaking under some burglar's foot.

Maybe I watch too many scary movies.

"I don't blame you for hating it when I was born," I tell her back, but the night is suddenly swirling around me. If I'd had my wits about me, I would have added, "I hated it, too." But that's the kind of thing you have to think up fast, or it's no good.

If I'd had my wits about me. That's what my dad always says. "If I'd had my wits about me, I would have told those clowns in marketing what I really thought of their sales plan." Or, "I should have spoken up about the broken soda machine in the employees' lounge. I would have, if I'd had my wits about me." Stuff like that.

It's as if my dad has been going through his life a couple of sentences too late. I don't like to say that, but it's true. He doesn't have very many friends— OK, any friends except for my mom, who isn't really his friend now. But that's all right, he can keep himself company any day of the week by repeating all the things he should have said.

Which makes for a lot of noise, even if it's only him doing the talking.

I usually do have my wits about me, but Lacey surprised me just now, saying that she hated it when I was born.

I guess if you had asked me the question "Does your beautiful, four-years-older sister love you? The way the sisters in *Little Women* love each other?" I would have said no. But she likes me OK, or so I thought.

I love *her*. I think.

So as I said, I was kind of surprised.

"I mean it, Ivy," Lacey tells me. Her voice sounds light, almost happy in the dark, as if we are having an ordinary conversation, the first normal one in this house tonight. Because our mother and father did *not* have an ordinary conversation after dinner. They had a fight.

Yeah, Mom finally opened her mouth—after one solid week of giving Dad the silent treatment. Ever since his big announcement.

Lacey and I never spoke to them about the silent treatment while it was happening. We never even talked to each other about it. I think that maybe we were afraid of what would happen next if we said anything.

I think that something bad is going to happen anyway—but to tell the truth, I'm so tired of Mom and Dad being mad at each other that I don't really care what they do anymore!

No, that's not true.

"I know you mean it, Lacey," I tell her back, even though that is not the truth, either. What I really want to say to my sister is, *Why are you being so awful all of a sudden? Why take it out on me, if you're in such a bad mood?*

Also, I would like to ask her if she means what she said.

But Lacey is already answering this last question when I haven't asked it yet, which I wasn't even planning to do.

"Before you were born, everything was perfect," she says, as if telling me a twisted bedtime story.

"No it wasn't. 'Nothing's perfect,'" I quote my dad again. He's always saying that, as if he is apologizing for something.

I can almost see my words rise up in the dark like rainbow-coated soap bubbles. They pop and disappear before they have floated across to Lacey's half of the room.

Lacey and I have this invisible line drawn down the middle of our bedroom floor, see, and I have to walk across her part of the room to go out the door. When I was little, Lacey used to charge me a penny if I wanted to leave—to go to the bathroom, for instance. "Pay the toll," she would tell me, and she would hold out her hand, palm up.

That got me for a while, but then I finally figured out that she had to walk across my part of the floor to get to her clothes in the closet. So that was the end of me paying the toll.

Lacey just turned fifteen. It's dumb that we have to share a bedroom, but we do. That's just the way it is. This is a two-bedroom house.

"We were the perfect family," Lacey continues, "Mom and Dad and me. All you have to do is look at the pictures in the scrapbook, and you can see what I mean. But then *you* came along."

It is her theory that I get all the attention in our family, but it is my theory that she does, and I can prove it—with that very scrapbook, in fact.

See, we have only one family scrapbook. The first few pages are full of pictures of people who are dead already, and then there are a couple of pages of Mom and Dad doing all kinds of fun stuff they never do now—such as skiing and getting dressed up for costume parties. I have to keep on reminding myself that I am related to these two people, they look so strange to me.

And then along comes about a hundred pages of Lacey.

I know I just said that nothing is perfect, but I was forgetting about Lacey. Perfect baby Lacey, with her shiny blond curls, her big dark eyes, and her smile—prettier even than Drew Barrymore's when she was a little girl in that movie, *E.T.* Baby Lacey's photographed smile seems to say, "Can you believe how cute I am?"

My mother and father look hypnotized in all the pictures of them holding Lacey.

I don't even wonder why. I don't blame my parents a bit, like I am trying not to blame Lacey for what she just said.

There are photographs showing baby Lacey at Christmas, Lacey at the zoo. Making a sand castle at the beach. At the zoo again. At Disneyland, shaking Minnie Mouse's hand. And then there's another photo, taken right after that, where she's getting a hug from Minnie.

I never even met Minnie Mouse.

Oh, and there's little Lacey—sitting in Dad's lap while he gets ready to blow out the candles on his birthday cake.

There is even a special black-and-white portrait of Mom and Lacey, each wearing a dark dress with a light collar. Maybe the dresses match, I can't remember the picture exactly. Except I do remember that Lacey's collar is frilly white lace. Naturally.

They used the picture for their Christmas card that year. The card is in the scrapbook, too. *Merry Christmas from the Millers!*

I close my eyes and pretend that I am turning the heavy pages of the scrapbook. I am looking for pictures of me.

Looking, looking.

Oh, there I am—on about page one hundred and two! Four blurry Polaroids of a funny-looking baby.

I look just about the same now, unfortunately. Frizzy brown hair that sticks out, and perfectly straight eyebrows that appear as if somebody drew them on my forehead with a ruler—not nice curved ones like Lacey's. And I have mud-brown eyes, Lacey recently informed me.

Well, at least they match my hair.

Why did Lacey have to get all the looks in the family? Couldn't I at least have gotten half of them? It's not fair. But no wonder there aren't that many pictures of me in our scrapbook.

I asked Mom about that once, and she laughed and pulled me in close for a hug. "Oh, honey—it's always that way with second babies," she said. "Moms and dads just run out of energy, that's all— and they forget to take as many pictures."

Huh.

Turn the next page of the scrapbook, and I'm two years old already. Happy birthday to me!

"Shut up," Lacey tells me in our darkened room.

"I didn't say anything."

"I could hear you whispering," she says. "It's like you were singing or something."

I take a deep breath and try to hold it so I won't accidentally whisper anything more that she can tease me about, because Lacey does like to tease. That's her specialty.

She's never been this mean to me before, though. In fact, up until fairly recently, I'd have said she was a great sister. For instance, last Christmas she took me shopping for Mom and Dad's presents when it was December twenty-third and I still did not have a clue what to get them.

"Music," she advised, steering me to the CD section for their era, the early 80s. "Because music is the gift of lo-o-ove," she added, which set us both off into a hysterical giggle-fit right there in the middle of Tower Records.

And then Lacey treated me to a slice of apple pie at Pie 'n' Burger. "Because apple pie is the gift of lo-o-ove," she crooned, rolling her eyes at me.

Which, naturally, led to another giggle-fit.

The gift of lo-o-ove. It doesn't seem as funny now.

I slowly let out the used-up air through my nose. And I am beginning to wonder, is that even Lacey over there? Because I saw this show on TV once where an alien took over someone's body and no one knew. Not for a long, long time.

"What—are you crying now?" Lacey asks in the dark. "Oh, poor little Ivy. Poor little Poison Ivy."

"Don't call me that," I say automatically for what is probably the eight-hundredth time.

"Poison Ivy, Poison Ivy!" she sings. "Your terrible big sister is teasing you again. Why don't you tell everyone, so they can feel sorry for you?"

"I don't want people feeling sorry for me." Which is another thing that maybe isn't true. I feel sorry for myself all the time. That's *my* specialty, I guess.

A second later, there is a knock on the door. It's probably Dad, coming to say good night. As if nothing happened earlier between him and my mom.

Oh, so that's the way it's going to be.

Dad opens the door a little and sticks his head in the room. "Are you guys asleep yet?" he asks. His bright whisper seems to bounce around the room like a pinball, escaped from some loser machine in an arcade.

"No, we're awake," Lacey whispers back. Because he probably heard us talking, so why lie?

"Well, night-night," he says.

"G'night, Dad," Lacey and I say back.

"Sleep tight," Dad adds, the way he always does.

"Don't let the bedbugs bite," the three of us call out together.

Dad blows a kiss into the room and then closes the door.

Lacey and I don't talk after that.

She hated it when I was born.

2
Hey

"HEY, ARE YOU GUYS GOING TO SPLIT UP?"
Lacey asks my mom at breakfast. Lacey licks peach
yogurt from her spoon as if she doesn't much care
what the answer is. But she cares, I can tell.

As usual, Dad has already left. If he went to work
any earlier, he'd have to wear his pajamas. The blue-
checkered quilt is folded neatly at the end of the
sofa, where he usually sleeps. His pillow is perched
on top like a crazy, oversized hat.

My mother gives a rusty little laugh. "We can't
afford to separate," she says. She walks over to the
sink and turns her back to us. She squirts soap into
the glass coffee pot and starts running hot water. She

sticks her finger into the stream of steaming water.

"Ouch," I want to yell for her. "Your finger's not a thermometer," I feel like scolding. But I stay quiet. Instead, I give Lacey a look that says, "See what you've done now?"

She sticks her tongue out at me. There are still some streaks of yogurt on it, too. Disgusting. "What do you mean, you can't afford it?" Lacey asks Mom. "Is that supposed to be a joke or something?"

"Or something," Mom says, turning around. She acts as if she is answering Lacey's question.

I stare at my mom. Her face still looks a little like the face of the pretty young woman in the first few pages of our scrapbook, except now it's bigger, redder, and shinier. Her hair is long, the same as before, only now, instead of being blond, it's kind of a faded color. Not white, exactly, but not blond. Somewhere in between.

She's a lot fatter, too. I hate to say it, but it's true.

"So, that's not a joke?" Lacey asks. "Do you mean that living apart would be too expensive?"

I want to tell her to stop, stop! But I also want to hear my mom's answer.

Mom lets out a sigh, as if she is a big, sad balloon that is leaking air. *Feeeep!* "Oh, honey, we're barely squeaking by in this house. How could we ever pay the bills for two different places?"

"But you do want to live apart," Lacey says, standing up suddenly. She is going to be late for summer school, but she doesn't even seem to care. She's making up a math class she got a D in last spring—and she's usually OK in math.

At least my grades are fairly good. Well, except for spelling.

My mother shrugs a little. "It doesn't matter what I want," she says, and she sighs again. Mom's a regular sighing machine lately.

"The money problem isn't all Dad's fault," Lacey says, as if that last sigh of Mom's was one too many. "He's doing the best he can, you know. And he'll get a raise when he takes that new job. If you *let* him take it, that is."

Dad's new job. He announced it a week ago. It would be in the same company, he told us, but it would mean a lot more responsibility. Which means a lot more work.

He looked proud as he told us his big news, but I knew he was nervous about how Mom would react.

See, she's been after him for ages to fix things at work so he could spend more time at home—even if it meant making a little less money. She was tired of him always working late, she said, and going into the office on weekends, leaving her with all the work around the house. Stuff like that.

And Dad promised he'd try to fix his schedule—someday, when the time was right.

So, now he was breaking that promise to Mom and then expecting her to congratulate him!

I can kind of understand why my mother got so mad at Dad that she stopped talking to him for a few days.

Mom looks frosty. "Whether or not your father accepts that position is entirely up to him. And you are way out of line talking to me this way."

Lacey's face turns kind of red. She is starting to look more like Mom, in fact. They've always looked alike, but in a good way.

"Maybe I should be the one to get a new job," Mom continues. "I'd just love to see how your father would like searching for a clean shirt each morning and sitting down to take-out food every night," she adds, narrowing her eyes.

"Susanna's mother works, and they don't eat very much take-out," I say. "Maybe you *should* get a job, Mom. It might be fun for you."

For some reason, Lacey looks as if she's about to faint. "But—but you can't just start working, boom, like that!" she sputters. And she jumps up, grabs her backpack, and starts heading for the door.

"Hold on a sec," my mom says, and Lacey freezes as if expecting the worst. "I want you to come home right after class today. I have an appointment, and I need someone to watch Ivy."

"*Mother*," Lacey squeals, shooting me a look. "But I had plans! With Mai!"

"I'll only be gone for an hour," Mom says. "Two at the most. And you can invite Mai to come home with you, if you want."

I stare into my cereal bowl. Seven Cheerios left.

"You are always doing this to me, Mother," Lacey complains, slamming her backpack onto the floor in a rage. "I am not dragging Mai over here again to help me take care of my sister. Ivy is almost twelve. She can take care of herself for a change. Even Dad thinks she's old enough to stay home by herself, at least during the day."

Oh great, I think, cringing. *Bring Dad into it, why don't you? That's just brilliant.*

Because, see, me staying home alone is another thing my parents disagree about.

When I turned eleven, my dad said he figured that I was old enough to stay by myself during the daytime if a responsible neighbor was home.

I guess Mrs. Pincus counts as a responsible neighbor. She's old enough to be considered responsible, that's for sure. But she is also a little strange. The most normal strange things she does are save teetering stacks of newspaper in her garage and to hang smudged old rubber bands around her kitchen doorknob until you almost can't turn it. "Just in case I need them some day," she always tells me.

I suppose if a bad guy ever trespassed in our yard, Mrs. Pincus could shoot rubber bands at him until he ran away crying.

Luckily, though, I haven't had to worry about this too much, because Mom knows I'm scared to stay home alone—no matter what my father says. So she makes Lacey stay with me.

Even if Mrs. Pincus is home.

Lacey swoops up her backpack and clutches it to her chest as if it is a life preserver. She heads out the door. "This is so—not—fair!" she shouts over her shoulder.

But she'll come right home after school anyway, I can tell.

I stir my last few Cheerios until they are able to circle the bowl all by themselves.

Mom stares, amazed, at the empty doorway. She is still holding the coffee pot as if she is about to pour a cup. A blob of soapsuds plops onto the floor.

It is as though I am invisible. I clank my spoon against the side of the cereal bowl to prove that I am still here.

It sounds as if I am.

3
Rearranging

SEVEN DAYS AGO, LACEY AND I WERE STILL friends, basically. Or at least I thought we were.

Six days ago, my parents had the big fight, and Mom told Dad he had to choose between the new job and her. And Lacey told me that she hated it when I was born.

Five days ago, Lacey asked Mom if they were going to split up, and Mom said no, they couldn't afford to.

Three days ago, Dad moved out, because Mom told him to choose, and he did. He's definitely accepting that new job. I guess my parents decided that they could afford a separation, after all—even though they're saying it's only for a while.

And last night, Lacey announced she is moving in with Dad.

I discovered this when I wandered into the bedroom to ask her if she wanted a cookie. She was heaping stacks of CDs and makeup on her bed next to some barely folded underwear.

"I'm outta here—I can't stand it anymore," she told me. "You'll just have to find another baby-sitter, Ivy, 'cause I'm moving in with Dad tomorrow morning. Anyway, where he lives is closer to my summer school."

It was as if she expected me to argue with her, but I just turned around and walked out the door without saying one single, solitary word.

Nobody has been saying much of anything, in fact, since last night. Lacey and Mom and I move through the house as though we are afraid that if we touch, we will knock the edges off each other.

No, wait—a noise! I am in the backyard playing with Nibby, my pet rabbit, but all of a sudden I can hear Mom yelling inside the house—at Lacey, who is trying to jam the most crucial of her many belongings into a medium-sized duffel bag. Dad already took the big one.

We are running out of duffel bags.

But let Lacey go, if she hates it here so much.

I mean, if parents can decide they don't have to live together, why can't sisters?

Maybe that's what Lacey and I need—a separation, just like Mom and Dad.

". . . young lady!" The last part of Mom's sentence bounces out of our bedroom window.

Lacey mumbles a reply.

And I can't help it, but the thought pops into my head. If Lacey moves out, I get my own room!

I squash my face into Nibby's soft black fur. He's a buck, which means he is a male. "I don't want Lacey to move away," I tell him. "Not really."

And that's true, because if Lacey goes, who'll be there to talk to me in that special sleepy way after we turn out the lights? Usually that's one of the best parts of the day. I love how we whisper back and forth, with more and more time passing between our murmurs as we get drowsy. I always wonder who's going to say the very last thing.

And the next morning, I can never remember who did.

I'll also miss hearing all the gross jokes that Lacey tells me, even if I don't always get them.

I'll miss hearing her breathe.

But one part of my brain is already rearranging the bedroom furniture. Like I said, I can't help it.

Nibby stops chewing on the grass for a second.

He is wearing his new red harness and leash, the ones Dad bought so that Nibby wouldn't keep on getting in trouble with my mother for making a mess. Getting all three of us in trouble, I mean— Nibby, me, and Dad. Because he's the one who gave Nibby to me two Easters ago.

Nibby stretches out his neck, chomps off a purple pansy as if killing flowers is his one and only job, and leaves it lying on the lawn.

"I told you, you're not supposed to do that," I scold. I stuff the pansy into my shorts pocket, along with all the other ones. "Don't wreck the flowers," I recite the rules, "and don't go to the bathroom on the grass."

You can train rabbits where to go. Supposedly.

As if on command, Nibby hunkers down and sticks his black tail out. His tail isn't puffy and round, like in the cartoons, but more like a fuzzy rectangle. Three tidy little droppings appear on the lawn.

I'm not going to put *them* in my pocket, that's for sure—even though they aren't really too terrible, not like dog doo. They can just stay there on the ground. "Quit pooping," I whisper.

Nibby turns his large bony head as if he is really listening to me. His big ears are sticking up, as usual, and the sun is shining through them. They look like gigantic leaves, almost.

Suddenly, Nibby springs straight up in the air and kicks out his hind feet. *Ka-poi-oi-oing!* When he lands, he lollops over to the juniper bush, with me behind him holding the leash. The juniper bush is his favorite. It's right outside my bedroom window.

"Shhh," I tell Nibby, but he hardly ever makes a sound. Just a growly, grunting noise sometimes when he's really nervous.

I know how he feels.

Nibby isn't growling now, though. He's digging. Dirt flies out from under him, and I step aside. He flops down into the long groove he has dug and crosses his hind feet like a lady at a tea party. He closes his eyes halfway. This is one relaxed rabbit.

I settle down next to him. He's going to be here for a while.

"I'm not mad at you, Mother," I hear Lacey's voice say extra patiently. But it is shaking a little.

"I refuse to let you leave this house, Lacey Miller," Mom tells her.

I'm not really eavesdropping—I'm taking care of my rabbit. It's not my fault the window is open.

"Well, Dad is going to pick me up any minute," Lacey says. "So you'll have to let me leave."

"I can't believe he didn't have the nerve to talk to me about this himself," Mom says. I hear a dresser drawer slam shut.

"It's OK," I whisper to Nibby. "Don't be scared."

"Maybe he tried," Lacey is saying. "Maybe that's why he left all those messages on the machine, asking you to call him."

"I have nothing to say to that man," Mom says, her voice flat.

"Well, that's just great, Mom," Lacey says. "First you say 'that man' should talk to you, then you claim you have nothing to say to him. That makes sense! I'm leaving. I'll go wait in front. Good-*bye*," she finishes, as if it is two words, not one.

I hear the bedroom door slam shut, and then everything is quiet in our bedroom.

In my bedroom.

Quiet, except for the sound of Mom crying.

I start to cry, too.

I can't help it.

4

RABBIT POOP

"LOOKS LIKE YOU'RE STUCK WITH ME, IVY,"
my mom says at dinner that night. The cardboardy
smell of take-out pizza fills the air, because leftover
pizza is still in its box in the oven.

I grab a bottle of orange salad dressing and start
shaking it, hard. *And you're stuck with me,* I feel like
saying back at her, but I don't.

"Want some more salad dressing?" I ask.

Mom shakes her head. "I'm not that hungry," she
says, her voice soft. She is acting as though she's just
too sad to eat.

I think about the four slices of pizza she's already
managed to choke down, but I don't say anything.

"Can I take some lettuce out to Nibby?" I ask instead.

Mom frowns when she hears Nibby's name. "I found some rabbit poop on the lawn this afternoon," she says, not answering my question. See, Nibby is supposed to go to the bathroom only in his hutch. There's a tray under the wire floor he stands on, and I pull the tray out a couple of times a week, dump his little messes in the trash, and then hose the tray clean.

I hold my breath, waiting for her to yell about the rabbit poop on the lawn. Mom complains a lot about my rabbit.

"I won't allow droppings all over my nice clean yard," Mom announces, right on schedule. She folds her arms to show me that she means business.

She won't allow this, she won't allow that. Who is she, the queen of what everyone else in the world is supposed to do?

"They're not all over the yard," I say.

"Don't argue with me, young lady," she snaps.

"Well, but, it's a big yard," I point out. And it's true. We have a small house but a big backyard. Why does Mom act as though the whole place is ruined if Nibby leaves his poop in one little spot?

She's like that about everything. If you spill grape juice on your second-best dress, for example, it's ruined—even if there are purple flowers already on the dress. Or if you get one little "Needs Improvement" on your report card, which has been known to happen in my case when it comes to spelling, then every good thing on that report card looks worse to Mom somehow.

And now she's doing the same thing with my dad. How could she let her anger over one stupid job wreck a whole, entire marriage?

On the other hand, I know the separation isn't all her fault. After all, Dad's the one who came up with that stunt about the new job. I'll bet he thought he could pull it off, too! That's the way he operates.

I hate to say that, but it's true.

For instance, my mom wanted to see this play at the Music Center for their last anniversary, but my dad didn't really want to go. I could tell. He said it sounded great, though, and that he'd get the tickets. Then he waited and waited, but he didn't buy them.

Mom asked him a couple of times if he'd gotten them yet, worrying that they'd sell out, but that just made him mad. "If you trusted me, you wouldn't even ask," he said.

He didn't call the box office until the morning of the performance, and they were all sold out by then, of course. "Sorry—I tried," he said, grinning a little apology.

It would probably be hard being married to someone like that.

"Ivy . . ." Mom is saying in a warning voice.

"OK, OK! I'll clean up the rabbit poop," I tell her.
"But you don't even know for sure that Nibby was
the one who—"

Mom gives me a look.

"OK," I repeat. "I'll tell him to use the toilet next
time."

"Don't get fresh with me, Ivy Miller, or there isn't
going to be a next time," Mom says, standing up.
Some greasy crumbs from the pizza crust bounce off
her faded USC sweatshirt.

I jump up, too. "Why, what are you going to do,
sit on him?" I ask. This is not a very nice thing to say,
since she is sensitive about her weight. But she's
threatening Nibby, who is the only one in the world
who understands me!

Mom's hand swings slowly through the air until
her finger is pointing to the hallway. "Go to your
room," she says, pronouncing each word carefully.

My heart is thudding. "Well, but first I have to
clean up—"

"Ivy, go to your room," she repeats, more slowly
this time.

"But—"

"This is the last thing I need right now," Mom says, shoving her chair under the table with a loud scrape.

"Well, what about me?" I yell. "What about what *I* need?"

"You need to go—to—your—room," Mom whispers.

And so I go, because there is such a scary look on her face.

My room. I guess it is my room now.

But it's funny how parents try to make their kid's bedroom so nice, with toys and games and fluffy pillows and stuffed animals and things in it, and then they say, "Go to your room!" when they want to punish you. As though they are sending you into a closet filled with black snakes.

I close the bedroom door with a soft click, shutting out the noise of my mother banging around in the kitchen. That is what she does when she wants to show my father how mad she is. Except he is gone, so I am her only audience.

And I refuse to listen!

I try to imagine what Dad and Lacey are doing right now. Still eating dinner? Washing the dishes?

I know that they're not watching TV, because Dad doesn't have a TV set yet. When I visited his apartment yesterday, he had only a card table with two folding chairs, a brand-new lumpy futon, and a sofa bed that some other guy left when he moved out. The guy who lived there before Dad.

I'd never sleep on a stranger's sofa bed. No way. Well, maybe Dad is letting Lacey sleep on the futon.

I wonder if *Dad* hated it when I was born. He sure didn't invite me to move in with him.

And that makes me feel bad.

I flop down on Lacey's fancy white bedspread without even taking off my grimy shoes. I think about what she said to me last week—that she hated it when I was born. "I hated it, too," I had wanted to tell her.

Would I have meant it? Am I sad I was born, or would that just have been a funny, sorry-for-myself thing to say?

Right now, I don't know the answer to that question. Things seem pretty bad, though.

I try to consider things from Lacey's point of view. She was four years old when I was born, and she'd always had things her own way—like a princess, maybe. But then I came along, and all of a sudden there were too many people in the family. That's probably what Lacey was talking about.

Maybe things just got a bit too crowded, and we couldn't afford to move to a bigger place. Not in

Southern California, anyway. At least that's what Dad always used to say.

But it's funny what grownups can really afford when they want something bad enough.

The one and only picture of Lacey in our scrapbook where she looks miserable, by the way, was taken the same month I was born. Her mouth turns down in that photograph, and there are little blue shadows under her eyes.

Even I almost feel sorry for her.

I kick off my shoes, then I scrunch my feet under Lacey's covers and pull her soft, yellow blanket up to my chin. This house feels cold all of a sudden, even if it is the middle of July in Southern California. We don't have air conditioning, either, and you really need it in Pasadena.

Well, there's one window unit in my mom and dad's room. Lacey and I used to hang out in there and play when I was little, when it got really, really hot. We called it The Cool Room. It was a fun place to be.

In fact, Lacey and I used to have a lot of fun together, now that I think about it! For my seventh birthday party, for example, when Lacey was eleven, she and her best friend, Mai, gave all us little kids manicures and beauty makeovers. Then they taught us a few dance moves. My friends thought I was so lucky to have a big sister. Even Susanna, my best friend, used to like her back then.

And it wasn't only birthdays. Lacey and I used to watch TV together—and cry whenever something sad happened on the screen. We loved to cry. Dad used to call us his little sobbers.

If it was a quiet show, sometimes I would fall asleep with my head on Lacey's lap.

The whole family would do fun stuff together in the olden days. We would hike up to Chantry Flats if it wasn't too hot out. My mom would pack a lunch for us.

Or Dad would pile all four bikes into the back of his van, and we'd drive down to Redondo Beach. Then we'd ride along the bike path, which goes on for miles, keeping an eye out for dolphins in the surf. Once, we even saw a California gray whale.

That was the same time I fell off my bike—which wasn't my fault. Lacey and I were way ahead of Mom and Dad on the bike path when these in-line skaters came racing along, all hunched over. Their elbows were flailing back and forth, like out-of-control swings. The skaters came up fast behind us, and they tried to pass me on the left.

Only they didn't allow enough room.

I swerved to the side—right into the sand and the red-edged ice plants that grow all along that path.

Clear, sticky goo oozed from the broken plants and mixed with the blood from my scrapes.

"You jerks!" Lacey shouted at the skaters, but of course they didn't hear. I still thought it was brave, though. She scrambled off her own bike to see if I was OK—which I was, basically, although I was trying hard not to cry.

Mom and Dad showed up, and Lacey helped me steer my bike up the steep concrete ramp as I limped along. And we went home early, but she never complained once about me wrecking things that day.

That's the way Lacey used to be.

That must have been in the spring, because that's when all the gray whales get together and migrate down to the Gulf of Mexico.

I guess what happened to our family eventually was that we kind of migrated in the opposite direction. Not to Alaska, I don't mean that—but apart.

I close my eyes and try whispering the words, just to hear how they sound: "I'm sorry I was ever born." I can almost picture myself slamming a door right after saying this. Only, in my daydream, I'm about fifteen years old, not eleven. Fifteen is when you should slam doors, I think. Lacey's age.

All at once, though, an image of Nibby hops into my daydream. Hey, what is he doing here?

Pretend-Nibby rubs his chin on a pretend-rock, marking it with his own personal rabbit scent that people can't smell, and then he looks at me. His ears stick up like special antennae that can tell the way I feel, which he can. It's really the truth! Well, not that Nibby's ears are antennae, but as I said before, he knows how I feel deep down inside.

He knows how mad I am at my mom and dad.

He knows how much I wish Lacey still liked me.

He knows that I wish I could be more like Lacey. Pretty and fun, and not so nervous about doorknobs turning and stairs creaking.

He knows how sorry I feel for myself—sorry because my parents are splitting up and my own sister can't stand living with me anymore.

And I know the way Nibby feels, too. Real-life Nibby needs me, that's the important thing.

If I were never born, who'd be taking care of my rabbit? Maybe someone who was mean. Or maybe no one! Maybe Nibby would just be a good-luck rabbit's foot on some horrible person's key chain!

I wish I could punch that person in the nose.

I wish I could punch *someone* in the nose. I hate to say that, but it's true.

Later, I hear Mom come creeping into my bedroom. She covers me up with an extra blanket, even though I am still in Lacey's bed. She brushes my hair back and kisses my forehead. She presses her cheek against mine for a second. Her skin feels cool, and she smells good, like—like Mom.

"Honey?" she whispers.

I wriggle down further under Lacey's covers, and I make a fake little I-am-asleep noise. *Mmmf-f-f.*

So Mom turns off the light, and then she leaves.

5

OH, SUSANNA

SUSANNA REID HAS BEEN MY BEST FRIEND since forever, and I'm lucky, because she lives only one block away. She and her family just got back from their summer vacation. They went to Lake Tahoe.

Some people's families go on vacation, and some people's families explode.

That's just the way it is.

Susanna has a pet rabbit, too, named Fuzz-Bunny. I took care of Fuzz-Bunny while Susanna was gone. We don't let Nibby and Fuzz-Bunny play together, though. We're pretty sure that Fuzz-Bunny is a doe, which means she is a female, and we don't want our rabbits to have babies.

No, that's not true—we would love them to have babies! But Mrs. Reid says nope, nothing doing, no way. And Susanna says that's a definite no.

We each do the translation for our own parents. If my mother says no, it means absolutely not. But just for today. Tomorrow might be another story, though, depending on the mood Mom is in.

If Dad says no, it means—well, he usually doesn't say no. Instead, he says, "That might not be such a good idea," or something vague like that. And then you can often get him to change his mind.

You can tell that my rabbit Nibby is a buck just by the way he acts, in my opinion. As a matter of fact, Fuzz-Bunny might be a buck, too, but that's another reason to keep our rabbits apart—because if they're both bucks, they'd fight.

Rabbits don't seem to know how to get together and just play. They're kind of like my mother and father that way. The way Mom and Dad are now, I mean.

When I walk up to Susanna's front door, there is a note taped to it. The note says, "We're in the back-yard." The Reids are known for doing this, and it drives me crazy. What if a burglar came to the door? They'd practically be inviting him in.

The Reids have never been robbed, but in my opinion, that just means they've been lucky. So far.

There is no sign of burglars this Saturday morning, though. Just Susanna and her mother, working in the rear garden. "Oh, hi, Ivy," Mrs. Reid greets me. "I thought you were Norman, back from the nursery. With the manure," she explains, brushing some hair out of her eyes. It's blond, like Susanna's hair—only darker.

Susanna laughs, and I can't help it, I start laughing, too. Susanna and I are like that when we're together. See, sometimes Susanna calls her father "Manure Man," because he loves gardening so much. But she only calls him that in private.

"It's just me," I say to Mrs. Reid. "No manure this time."

I am a little worried that Mrs. Reid is going to put me to work in the garden, because she likes to say, "Many hands make light work." Usually I wouldn't mind. But today I want to talk with Susanna—in private.

It's as though Mrs. Reid knows this, because she says, "Susie-Q, why don't you dump these dead-heads on the compost heap and then go inside with Ivy and make some lemonade?"

Susanna starts laughing again—probably at the word "deadheads." Susanna picks up the basketful of snipped-off flowers, and we walk over to the compost bin, which is Mr. Reid's hobby, practically.

The Reids' compost bin is way in the back of their yard. It is divided into three big wire boxes, and we dump the snipped-off flowers on top of the pile of debris in the first box.

I hold my nose, even though it really doesn't smell too bad. But it looks like it smells terrible. "I don't get it, how all this junk turns into something good for the garden," I honk. My voice sounds funny because I am squeezing my nose.

And I *don't* get it, but there's the proof, right in front of me: Everything in the first box starts to crumble, and it's tossed into the second box by Manure Man and his trusty pitchfork. Then that stuff crumbles even more, and Mr. Reid tosses it into the third box.

And when that finishes crumbling, you have compost, or "black magic," as Susanna's parents call it. They feed it to their plants along with the manure, for dessert, I guess, and their plants just go nuts.

The stuff smells like a walk in the forest by then, so that part's OK.

"It's the wonder of nature," Susanna tells me, doing her best imitation of her mom.

We both laugh some more, but I stop first, and quicker than usual.

"What's the matter?" Susanna asks me.

I gulp, not even wanting to say the words aloud.

But finally I do. "Oh, Susanna—my dad moved out, and Lacey's living with him now."

Susanna stares at me, stunned. "I was only gone a week," she finally says. "When did all this happen?"

"Just a couple of days ago," I say.

"And Lacey moved out, too?" she asks, sagging against the compost bin as if some of the air has gone out of her.

"I just told you," I snap, and then I try to make a joke of it. "I get to be alone—at last."

The thing is, though, Susanna is an only child. She has always wished she had a big sister, so it's sometimes hard for her to understand what the big deal is when I complain about Lacey.

Until the last few months, anyway.

But even Susanna has not been exactly crazy about my big sister lately, since Lacey's teasing has gotten so much worse. Especially when Susanna comes over. "The tiny twins," Lacey called us last time, because basically we still look like a couple of kids. Which we are. What's wrong with that?

"Why don't you guys just grow up?" Lacey said that day, scowling as she checked her lipstick in the mirror. Then she raced out the door to go hang out with Mai in Old Town.

Lacey seems to have this thing lately about me growing up.

Susanna knocks dirt from the basket and slowly shakes her head. "It's not funny, Ivy. If your parents get divorced, you'll be a kid from a single-parent home."

A single-parent home! I hadn't thought about that. There's always stuff about kids from single-parent homes in magazines and newspapers. And whenever some teenager steals a car and makes the police chase him for a hundred miles on the freeway, the TV reporters look serious and say, "It is alleged that he comes from a single-parent home."

I try to imagine myself stealing a car.

I try to imagine even being able to see over the steering wheel—because I am kind of short, basically. Susanna is too, which is probably one of the reasons we are such good friends.

"You might even have to sell your house and move away," Susanna says, eyes wide.

"Thanks a lot," I tell her. But now, I'm really getting worried.

"Oh, Ivy, lots of parents get divorced," Susanna says, swiftly changing her point of view to make me feel better—which is what friends are supposed to do. "Remember our class last year? Jennifer Borden's parents split, but her life is still perfectly normal."

I try to remember our fifth-grade class. "Yeah," I say gloomily. "But think of Karl Henniger."

Susanna makes a face, which is easy to do whenever you think about Karl Henniger, because he is a really mean kid—and strange, too. He brought a dead bird in once to share with the class.

And he is from a single-parent home.

"You're not like Karl Henniger," Susanna says. "You're much more like Jennifer."

"Maybe I am like Karl," I say. I pinch my fingers together and pretend that I am holding up Karl's dead bird. "I found this in my backyard," I say. "I think the cats got to him." Then I give a ghastly, Karl-like grin.

Susanna swings the basket at me. "Quit it," she says, but she is laughing.

"Ouch!" I say, being Ivy again.

Susanna shakes her head a little. "But it's weird, isn't it, how parents can be married one day and then, *abracadabra,* they're divorced?" Susanna says. "That's so sad."

"You keep saying that they're getting a divorce," I complain. "They're not. My mom says they're just separated."

"Separated," Susanna says, trying out the word as if it is brand new. She shakes her head and hooks a blond curl behind one of her ears. "I don't know, Ivy—it sounds like Divorce City to me," she says, looking serious.

"Well, it's not Divorce City," I say flatly. "It's only Separation Town."

Susanna stares down at her muddy sneakers, then a crafty smile appears on her face. "You should try to get them back together," she says. "I'll bet you could do it—or we could. It'd be fun! We could think up something that would make your dad all jealous, maybe, and then he—"

"—then he would come back home? And we'd all live happily ever after?" I say, sounding kind of sarcastic, but I can't help it. If my father did come back home, then what?

Another million years of almost-slammed doors, of folded-up quilts on the sofa?

Not to mention the silent treatment?

I'm exhausted just thinking about it.

Susanna's getting all *Parent Trap*-y on me at the exact time I need her most.

I need her to be my friend. I need her to listen to me talk—about Lacey, I realize suddenly, not about my mother and father. Because, to tell the truth, it felt weirder to have Lacey move out than it did when Dad left.

I hate to say that, but it's true.

Susanna just looks confused, though. "Don't you want to live happily ever after?" she asks.

I think about this for a moment. *Who doesn't?* I feel

like asking her. It's just that I don't exactly know what I mean by "happily ever after" anymore.

But I can't say this out loud, or Susanna might think I'm weird.

Like Karl Henniger.

6

FAMILY-STYLE

IT IS ANOTHER SATURDAY, TWO WEEKS LATER, and my parents are together at a coffee shop. I'm home alone, out in the backyard with Nibby.

Susanna is shopping with her mom. I don't know where Lacey is. Now that she's living with my dad, Mom can't make her stay with me anymore.

I feel safer outside than indoors when no one else is home. You don't hear so many spooky noises when you're outside, for one thing, and it would be easier to run away if anything bad happened.

I don't know what Mom and Dad are talking about at the coffee shop. Probably something to do with all the late-night phone calls they've been making to each other. But Susanna should not be getting her hopes up about my parents moving back in together, I know that much.

I couldn't hear what my mom was saying on the phone the one time I happened to overhear her end of a call, and I wasn't sure I wanted to. But Mom's low, angry voice uncoiled down the hall like the yellow smoke from one of those stinky Fourth of July tablets that you light on the sidewalk—the ones that turn into long, ashy worms and then blow away in a second, leaving a black mark that lasts for the rest of the year.

I have a very bad, black-mark feeling about this Saturday afternoon.

I stroke Nibby's ears back. He loves it when I do that! His ears feel hot and wonderful under my cool fingers. I rub my hands through my own hair, pretending I have ears like that. It would be kind of great—if everyone else had them, too, I mean. Not just me. I wouldn't like that.

I hear Mom's car chug down the driveway and sputter to a stop. It makes a final little noise sometimes when she turns it off, as though it's trying to show my mom how exhausted it is after doing all that driving.

The car door slams. "OK, back you go," I whisper to Nibby, and I pick him up—carefully, so he won't scratch me if he kicks. He doesn't mean to do that, but it happens sometimes. And you can't tell a rabbit not to kick. Kicking comes with the rabbit.

"I'm home," my mom calls out to me from the driveway.

"I know," I answer. "I'll be right in." I stuff Nibby into his hutch and tear off a hunk of alfalfa hay for him to eat. He mostly eats rabbit chow, but also hay—and a few little treats, but not too many. Bananas are his favorite.

Rabbits have very delicate stomachs.

I think I'm beginning to have a delicate stomach, too. The tuna sandwich I ate for lunch feels as though it is doing somersaults somewhere right under my heart.

Mom is pouring a glass of lemonade when I walk into the kitchen. "Want some?" she asks.

"I guess," I say, a little reluctantly. If I said no, she'd probably take my temperature, because I am not known to turn down snacks.

"Wash your hands—after touching that rabbit," she tells me.

"I was just about to," I say. My mother is always telling me to do stuff that I was just about to do, and I hate it.

No wonder Lacey moved out, a tiny voice inside me says.

Mom sighs as she sets the two glasses on our kitchen table, showing me that she expects me to sit down with her and talk. But I don't feel much like talking.

I sit down anyway.

"So, I saw your father this afternoon," she says.

"Yeah, you told me you were going to. Before you left," I say.

But she's not listening to me. In fact, the way she's acting reminds me of when you're swimming with a friend, and you try to yell stuff at each other underwater. It's as though my mother has to finish what she is saying before she runs out of air. "We decided that we should have dinner together tonight, the four of us," she says.

I look up from my hands, which are gripping my sweaty lemonade glass. Is my heart still beating?

Could Susanna actually have been right? Are my parents getting back together?

"Ivy? Are you OK?" Mom asks, leaning forward.

"I'm fine," I say, but my voice does sound funny.

"Take a sip," Mom urges me, still concerned. "Breathe."

I swallow a gulp of lemonade and clear my throat as if I had a tickle there.

"So, be ready at six o'clock, all right?" Mom says.

I nod my head, afraid to say a word.

"We've decided to get a divorce," my dad informs Lacey and me.

I look around the crowded restaurant. The people nearby seem extra colorful all of a sudden, as if they are in a movie.

Separation Town is fading away, fast. It's Divorce City for us.

This is called a family-style restaurant, which means kids are allowed to be a little noisy, but still, you can't just run screaming from the table. That is probably why our parents brought us here to give us this news.

But running away screaming is exactly what I feel like doing.

"It's not a separation anymore," my mother says, as if she needs to explain. "We want to make that perfectly clear to you girls, because I think things have been a little confusing lately."

"For Ivy, maybe. Not for me," Lacey says crisply.

Me? Confused?

Everyone turns to look at me. I wish I could turn to look at me.

The truth is, I don't know where to look.

"Thank you," Dad says, speaking to the waitress, who has appeared out of nowhere. Plates of food are balanced on her arm as if she is about to perform a juggling act. Everyone at the table is embarrassed.

We hold our breath while the waitress sets our plates carefully in front of us. I look down at my hamburger, coleslaw, and fries.

My stomach twizzles up.

Finally, having sensed that we are obviously in the middle of an important family discussion—to put it mildly—the waitress flees.

Dad ignores his spaghetti and meatballs, and Mom doesn't start eating her meatloaf, either. But Lacey digs right in. She squirts ketchup on her hamburger, slaps the bun shut, lifts it, and chomps down hard. She swallows. "Delicious." Lacey is being sarcastic, but Mom and Dad let her get away with it.

Dad clears his throat as if he wants to start over. "Our problems have nothing to do with you two kids," he says.

"Nothing," Mom echoes.

Maybe it's Nibby's fault, I think, wishing I could be the one to say something sarcastic for a change.

"Well," Lacey says, shrugging, "why don't you go see a marriage counselor, then? Other parents do. They don't just run away from each other when they have one little fight."

Mom rearranges her fork, knife, and spoon so that they line up perfectly. "First of all, it wasn't only one little fight. And second, what makes you think that we haven't been seeing a counselor?"

Lacey is so surprised that she actually stops eating for a second. "You have?" she finally says.

Mom and Dad both nod. "For the last couple of months," my father says. "We don't tell you kids everything."

Everything? They don't tell us *anything*.

"But—but—why isn't it working?" Lacey asks, slapping her hand on the fake wood table with a muffled clank. She has a ring on each finger, and one on her thumb, too. All of them glitter angrily.

My mom shakes her head a little. "Maybe we put it off too long. Or maybe it *is* working," she says. "Maybe it's kind of like when people say their prayer isn't being answered, only it is—the answer is no."

"We don't even go to church," Lacey reminds her coldly.

"It was only a comparison," Mom says, keeping her voice steady.

"Well," I ask, also trying to sound calm, "has this counselor pointed out to you how dumb it is to split up over a stupid job?"

Dad straightens his fork. "The fight over the job was just a symptom of much bigger problems. You know, like a runny nose is a symptom of a cold?"

"What?" Lacey squawks. She looks as if she's going to jump up any minute and start running around in circles like Daffy Duck, restaurant or no restaurant.

"The fight was the tip of the iceberg," Dad says, trying to explain it better.

"Well, what's the iceberg, then?" I say. "Fix that!"

"Yeah. Fix the iceberg," Lacey chimes in.

"If we could, we would," Mom tells us. "But some things just aren't meant to be."

Lacey shoots her a look. "You don't have to sound so calm about everything, Mother. Don't you know what a mess this is going to make out of all our lives? I, for one, do not need this hassle right now." She pauses. Then she blurts out, "You guys are so selfish!"

I can barely believe my ears, that Lacey would have the nerve to say these things. Dad and Mom seem pretty amazed, too.

Hah! It serves them right, in a way. Like I said before, I'll bet they decided to take us out to this restaurant for their big news because they knew we wouldn't throw a fit in public. But now *they* can't throw one, either—even if Lacey deserves it.

"I'm quite aware that we're all going to have to make some sacrifices, Lacey," Mom says, sounding a little shaky. "For instance, I'm going in for career counseling first thing next week. I already have an appointment, in fact. Not that finding a job is going to be easy for me." Sigh.

Lacey looks as if someone just shot her with an

arrow, but all she says—or whispers, really—is, "You're getting a job. Perfect."

"Lacey," Dad says in his warning voice.

"And furthermore," Mom continues, "I'm also aware that I . . . I . . ."

Her voice trails off, and her eyes fill up with tears. Dad reaches over and pats her hand, which somehow hurts me so much that I can't look.

So I shut my eyes.

"Your mother is going to be fine, just fine," he tells Lacey and me. "This is a tough period for us all, but when the two of us talked this afternoon, we realized that we weren't making things any easier for you two by not being honest about the situation."

"Oh, great," a pale Lacey says. "Thank you for your honesty. It makes things less confusing for Poison Ivy, I'm sure."

"You know what? *I* want a divorce!" I hear myself announce over the top of my own hamburger.

All of a sudden I have everyone's attention.

"What?" Dad says, looking as if I just said something in German—or maybe even Russian.

"You heard me," I say as coolly as I can. "I want a divorce. From Lacey." I can't believe I didn't think of it before—we're already separated, so why shouldn't we get a divorce?

Lacey snorts. "Huh! Well, I want a divorce from

you. So what do you think about *that*, Poison Ivy?"

"Girls," Mom says, and Dad looks around the restaurant nervously.

Oh, so *now* they're worried about what people might think?

Mom shakes her head as if trying to rearrange her thoughts. "But why on earth—?"

Lacey pounds the table with her fist. "Because Ivy's a big baby, and she knows I can't stand her anymore, that's why!" she says.

People around us are starting to stare. "Thanks for clearing that up for everyone," I tell Lacey.

"We're getting a little off the subject," Dad says, like someone trying to regain control of an unruly PTA meeting.

"Off *your* subject, maybe. Not mine," I say.

For a second I wonder what in the world is making me utter these words—out loud, anyway. But who cares? It feels great!

My mom tries a different approach with me now. "Honey, you can't divorce your sister."

"That's right," Lacey says, sarcastic once more. "Divorces are only for mommies and daddies, sweetie pie."

"Shut up," I tell her.

"You shut up."

"Girls."

I turn my back on Lacey. "Why can't sisters officially split up if they want to?" I am trying to sound logical. "We have problems of our own. And they have nothing to do with you two parents," I add, inspired once more as I echo Dad's own words.

He looks as if he is trying to remember why they sound so familiar.

"So why can't Lacey and I get divorced?" I repeat. "You heard her say she can't stand me anymore," I explain, spelling it out for my parents—and anyone else who might be listening.

"Well, that's no big news flash. I never liked you," says Lacey. "Not when I was four years old, and you pooped in your diapers all the time. Not when I was eight, and you gave me chicken pox and made me miss being Sacagawea in the class play. Not when I was ten, and Mom and Dad made me drag you along whenever I wanted to go to the mall with a friend. And not last year, when they made me invite you to my birthday party in Old Town. What a treat that was."

I ignore all this. "And Lacey moved out on me, didn't she?" I say to my parents. "Just the way Dad moved out?"

"That's enough, Ivy," Dad says. His voice is quiet, as usual, but even I know when to shut up.

The table is silent for a moment, though the air

still seems to ring with our angry words.

"Well," Mom says, "that brings up another point, as it happens. Your father and I also thought we should talk more openly to you girls about our present living arrangements."

"Yes, our living arrangements," Dad repeats.

"We just kind of fell into this thing about you staying with your father, Lacey," Mom continues. "But it's only for the summer."

"I want to live with Dad permanently," Lacey says, narrowing her eyes. "And I don't want to live with *her*." She jerks her thumb in my direction.

"Well," my father says to Lacey, "that's something your mother and I will decide once summer school is over."

"You can't expect me and Lacey to live together if we're getting a divorce," I say, trying to sound reasonable.

Mom and Dad stare at us, and then they stare at each other. It's as if they are asking, *How did this happen?*

"Please pass the ketchup," I say, businesslike.

"Your noodles are getting cold," Lacey tells Dad.

And so we all eat our delicious dinners.

7

Gardening

MY MOM SAYS THAT SHE AND I ARE GOING TO have a big Sunday breakfast if it kills her. A family breakfast. But are we even a family anymore? It's just the two of us.

Mom is standing at the stove flipping pancakes. She made me get up when it was still dark, practically. Either my mother woke up really, really early, or she never went to sleep last night. But she looks just as tired whichever way.

"Pour the juice, would you?" Mom says, waving her spatula in the direction of the refrigerator. "There are some clean glasses in the dishwasher."

"OK," I say, trying not to yawn.

"And then see if you can find some nice flowers outside for the table," Mom says, pasting a fake bright smile on her face. "If Nibby hasn't eaten them all, that is."

Uh-oh. I don't want her to get mad at my rabbit. He didn't do anything. He's still asleep, probably. Lucky Nibby.

"We might as well have a little bouquet to brighten up our breakfast table," Mom says. She gives me another everything's-perfect grin.

I hate this. I wish she wouldn't creep me out first thing in the morning.

And flowers on the table? When our family has broken into pieces the day before?

"OK," I say again, matching her smile. "I think there are some of those yellow-y ones left. And some pansies," I add, just as I remember that Nibby probably nipped off the last one a week ago. "I'll find something," I say, sounding a little desperate. I slosh some orange juice into two glasses, jam the juice container back into the refrigerator, and run out the back door.

It is very early, but Nibby wakes up and sees me right away. He starts hitting his metal food cup against the wire-mesh sides of his hutch, sending the food that was left in the cup flying all around. *Bang, bang, bang.* Nibby is a rabbit who has never missed a meal in his life, but he's sure that he's about to.

"I'll feed you in a second," I call out to him softly, and he glares at me.

I grab the few flowers that Nibby has left standing and break off the leafy ends of some camellia branches to plump up the arrangement a little.

Inside the house, I cram the leaves and flowers into a vase and plunk it down on the kitchen table. Then I scoot back outside to feed Nibby.

Inside again, panting a little, I wash up, dry my hands on my pajamas, and sit down. "Mmm," I say, looking at the pancakes.

"Help yourself."

We eat silently for a moment, while I watch a little red spider crawl out from under a flower petal and onto a leaf. He stops and seems to look around our kitchen, confused.

I know exactly how he feels.

"I'm going to have to run some errands this afternoon at about two o'clock," Mom says after taking a sip of her juice. "You can go play over at Susanna's while I'm gone."

There are a lot of things wrong with that sentence. First, Susanna and I don't play. We haven't played since we were about eight years old. We hang out together now. And second, while I haven't exactly been trying to avoid Susanna, I am not about to go out of my way to see her, now that my parents are officially getting a divorce.

OK, maybe I *have* been trying to avoid Susanna. Divorce City, she called it. Well, I guess that's my unofficial address from now on, and I might as well get used to it.

Susanna would never understand how weird I feel about Lacey moving out, though. Even I don't really understand it.

Basically, I can't talk to Susanna about Lacey leaving, and I can't talk to her about the divorce. Because what if Susanna gets so weirded out about Divorce City that she doesn't want to be friends with me anymore? I mean, if a dad and a sister can leave a person, then why not a best friend?

No, I can't risk that.

But it's terrible when all of a sudden there's something you can't talk to your best friend about. I could be mad at Mom and Dad and Lacey for that alone, if for no other reason.

I don't feel like explaining all this to my mom, though. She's got enough problems.

"A penny for your thoughts," Mom says around a mouthful of pancake.

I grin weakly. "Why can't I just stay home?" I ask. "I'll call Mrs. Pincus if I get scared or something," I promise, but I cross my fingers under the table.

Because—yeah, right! Mrs. Pincus, who calls me over to her kitchen window just about every day so she can read me my astrological forecast because we're both Libras, is probably a lot stranger than any stranger who might come to the door.

I'll take my chances, thanks. I'll just stay outside in the backyard with Nibby.

"Mrs. Pincus went to visit her sister in Hesperia," Mom says, helping herself to another pancake. "I told Cheryl you'd be over at around two."

Cheryl. That's Mrs. Reid.

I can hear my heart beating in my ears. "But I don't want to go over to Susanna's," I say, trying to sound calm. "I'm not in the mood. How about if I promise to call Mrs. Reid if anything weird happens here while you're gone? Or—I know! I'll come help you run the errands. I can carry stuff." I seem to be talking faster and faster. Next thing you know, I'll be making those little grunting noises and chewing on a towel the way Nibby does when he's nervous.

Mom looks at me curiously. "What in the world?" she finally asks, after taking a sip of coffee. "Anyone listening to us talk would think that you and Susanna Reid weren't best friends anymore!"

"Well, people do change," I mumble. My mom and my dad changed, didn't they? Why is this such a hard concept for Mom to grasp?

Mom laughs and shakes her head. "Oh, Ivy. You are too much."

"Hello, stranger!" Mrs. Reid greets me at the foot of her driveway, peeking over the top of the gigantic clump of plants she's holding. Pale, tangled roots trickle dirt onto her gardening shoes, but she doesn't seem to notice.

Mrs. Reid is kneeling next to a hole she has just dug in her front-yard garden, and a worm is poking through the dirt at one side of the hole. He is waving around in the air as if to say, "Hey, what the—?"

"Hi, Mrs. Reid," I murmur, feeling shy for some reason. Probably because she called me "stranger." "What are you doing?"

"Dividing this plant," she says, shifting the clump a little in her arms as she speaks.

"Dividing it?" I ask blankly.

"I'll show you," she says eagerly, and she leads me over to an old feed bag that is lying on the lawn. "Phew!" she exclaims, placing the heavy clump on the bag. She sits back on her heels and tries to wipe her brow with her shoulder.

I look around for Susanna, but I don't see her. Well, that's good.

"She's in the backyard," Mrs. Reid says, before I even ask the question. "Grab that knife, would you?"

Relieved that I don't have to figure out what to say to Susanna right away, I pick up a long, sharp knife that was resting on the feed bag and hand it to Mrs. Reid. "What are you going to do, *scare* the plant to death?" I joke.

Mrs. Reid grins. "Nope. I'll use the knife, which I sterilized in boiling water, to divide this big clump into sections. Then we can replant the sections."

"How come you sterilized the knife?" I ask.

"To kill any germs that might be on it," Mrs. Reid says. "I don't want to infect the roots. Dividing them is stressful enough."

Mrs. Reid usually seems to know what she is talking about, but I have to admit that I am thinking it is a little unlikely that a shiny knife could infect what is basically just a bunch of dirt. But I don't question her. "Stressful," I echo, nodding in what I hope is a wise way. "But how come you have to divide the plant in the first place?"

"Because its flowers have been getting smaller every year, and skimpier, too," Mrs. Reid says, frowning a little. "And this way, we'll end up with five or six healthy plants instead of one worn-out one. I'll even give you a couple to take home!"

"Thanks," I say, already thinking of where I might put them. Somewhere safe from Nibby, that's the important thing.

Mrs. Reid pulls gently at the leaves all the way down to the dirt, as if she is parting the plant's hair. She is deciding where to cut, I guess. Then she starts sawing away with the knife. About a third of the clump falls off onto the feed bag. "That's good," she says to herself. "Now, you grab the root ball and pull it apart, Ivy. Gently."

"But I don't know how," I object. "I don't want to wreck anything."

"You won't. It's really pretty sturdy, after all," she assures me.

And so I pick up the root ball and start to pull. After a second or two, when it feels as though nothing is going to happen, the root ball suddenly starts to come apart, sort of like two hands unclasping.

"Bingo," Mrs. Reid says, beaming. "Now, if we're lucky, they'll make two perfect plants."

Bingo!

The cool thing about gardening is that you get to start something and then finish it all in the same day—such as dividing these plants. And there's always something to look forward to, like watching stuff grow.

"Oh, there you are!" a voice exclaims.

It's Susanna, and my troubles come flooding back, filling the warm space in my heart where thoughts about gardening used to be.

8
WHAT'S THE DIFFERENCE?

"**So, what's the difference between** compost and garbage?" I ask Susanna a few minutes later. We're in her backyard, and I am trying to get a conversation going before she can ask me anything about my parents. Because I am not a very good liar.

Susanna is using a pitchfork to turn over the mucky stuff in the second and third wire boxes in the compost bin.

Fuzz-Bunny is hopping around like mad, rubbing her chin on anything that sticks up. She hops over to me and rubs her chin on my sneaker. She tries nibbling on the edge of the rubber sole for a second before giving up and dashing away.

Susanna pauses and wipes a strand of sandy-colored hair back with one arm. Her face is pink and sweaty, because this is a hot, hot day. "Well," she says slowly, blinking bright blue eyes, "they're both stuff that you normally throw away."

"Yeah, but what's the *difference?*" I ask again.

"I guess that garbage is bones and meat scraps and used-up Kleenexes and icky junk like that," she tells me. "It's stuff that—oh, I guess it rots and everything, but it would stink if you tried to save it. And it would be unsanitary. You never put things like that in a compost heap," she adds, sounding instructive.

"How come this isn't unsanitary, then?" I ask, pointing to the Reids' bin. I can see a couple of banana peels in the first wire box in the bin. They are poking out from under a big, wet lump of grass clippings. And there are coffee grounds on the grass, and rabbit droppings on the coffee grounds, like nuts sprinkled on some gross kind of sundae.

"It just isn't," Susanna says, flipping another forkful of compost. "This is all, like—natural stuff," she explains. "Even rabbit poop is natural, because Fuzz-Bunny only eats grass and things like that."

"Well, meat is natural, isn't it?"

Susanna shakes her head. "No, not in a compost heap. It would wreck it. Fuzz-Bunny, you come back here," she yells suddenly.

"You cwazy wabbit," I shout, too, doing my best Elmer Fudd imitation.

Susanna laughs and leans the pitchfork against the bin, and we scramble off to round up Fuzz-Bunny, who has sneaked into the Reids' vegetable garden—which is off-limits to her.

"Uh-oh," Susanna says to me, keeping her voice low as we see a lettuce leaf topple. "If Manure Man finds out, I'll have to listen to that lecture again. The one about responsible pet ownership. Maybe you and I both will."

"Yikes," I whisper back. "Here, bunny-bunny-bunny." I crouch down and reach out my hand as if I am holding a piece of banana. "Look, Fuzz-Bunny—yum!"

Fuzz-Bunny is usually pretty easy to catch. She is a small, lop-eared rabbit and very sweet, not a tough guy like Nibby. But sometimes she has a mind of her own, and this is one of those times. She sees me lurching forward in a kind of duckwalk, still bent over. She springs straight up in the air and turns around before she even lands.

"Gotcha," Susanna exclaims, grabbing the bolting rabbit by the scruff of the neck.

Fuzz-Bunny gives a couple of pretty good kicks before Susanna cuddles her close. Then Susanna murmurs a few words into Fuzz-Bunny's soft, floppy ears and tucks her safely into the hutch.

Susanna must already have cleaned it. There's fresh water, a bowl of rabbit chow, a carrot, and a clean towel waiting inside. "Bad rabbit," I pretend-scold.

"She doesn't know any better," Susanna says. "Come on," she says, and we trudge back to the compost bin.

I sink down near the bin, my back against the fence, and watch Susanna work. "What's wrong?" she asks, not looking at me.

Whoa. "What do you mean?" I ask, stalling.

"Since when do you care two hoots about compost? Or one hoot?" she asks back.

I look down at my hands. "Since never," I admit—even though I do like gardening, as I said before. At the Reids', I mean. Not at home.

"So, what's wrong?" she repeats. "It's your parents, right? They're getting a divorce."

Double whoa! I might as well have the bad news written on my forehead in fluorescent ink. "Yeah," I mumble. "We all had dinner last night."

"Together?"

I nod glumly. I don't want to look at Susanna, so I stare down at the grass.

The Reids have some very interesting grass here.

"But why didn't you tell me right away?" Susanna wants to know.

"I don't know. I guess I didn't want to say the words out loud."

Susanna sits down next to me and puts a grubby hand on my arm to comfort me. "Maybe it won't be so bad," she says. "At least it's happening in July," she adds, as if she has just found the bright side.

"What's so great about July?"

"Well, I mean you won't have to announce it to everyone at school. By the time classes start, it'll be old news."

"Yeah," I say. "And it'll be a new school, too." Sure enough, things are looking a little better. I'm pretty lucky to have a friend like Susanna. "Do your parents fight?" I ask her after three or four heartbeats.

"Sure they do," she says, her voice soft, as she rubs some dirt from her chin.

"What do they fight about?" This is not the kind of thing we usually talk about, so I am feeling a little weird.

But Susanna doesn't seem to mind my nosiness. "Oh, I don't know," she says, thinking. "What movie to see? Whether or not to go to a party?" It sounds as though she is asking questions, not answering them.

"No," I say. "I mean their big fights. What are those like?"

"I guess they don't have them. Not in front of me, anyway," she says, brushing her hair back again. "I mean, I do hear them talking sometimes at night. Extra-loud. But they're always OK by the morning." Susanna is frowning now, she's thinking so hard.

"Huh," I say. "My parents were never OK in the morning after they had a fight. They just clammed up and tried to stay out of each other's way. Finally, Mom just stopped talking altogether."

"Well, I know one thing," Susanna says, brightening. "My mother told me once that *her* mother and father had a rule about never going to sleep while they were still mad at each other. Maybe my mom and dad do that."

I think about it. "If my mother and father had tried that, they never would have gotten any sleep at all," I say.

Susanna sighs and picks up a twig. We watch an ant climb to the top of the twig and down the other side. "I guess it wouldn't work for all parents," says Susanna. "But one thing's for sure, my parents never clam up. They talk about everything, all the time. Maybe, when they fight, they just get so tired of talking that they forget what they were mad about in the first place. All that talk is boring," she finishes.

I laugh a little. "It sounds like your parents are compost people, and my parents are garbage people."

Susanna looks a little shocked. "That's kind of harsh," she says.

"No, no," I say, trying to explain. "I only mean that when my parents fight, it's like they're just throwing garbage at each other. They yell and say terrible things, but they never get anywhere. Your parents talk instead of yelling. They turn the problem over and over till they're sick of the whole thing, and then they're ready to do something else."

"Compost people," she says, thinking about it.

I draw a line in the dirt with my finger. It hasn't rained in months, and the ground is dry.

I take a deep breath and stare at my finger as it makes another line, a parallel one. Suddenly I blurt out, "Here's the thing, Susanna. I can't talk to you about Lacey, because you guys don't like each other anymore," I say. "And I can't tell you how I feel about my parents getting a divorce, because it makes you so uncomfortable."

Susanna has seemed to shrink a little as I speak.

"I like Lacey," she protests, but her words are not very convincing. "And talking about divorce doesn't make me uncomfortable."

"Come on. Don't lie," I challenge her. "Let's face it—this whole mess might mean we can't be friends anymore."

"What might mean we can't be friends? Your parents splitting up?" Susanna looks confused.

"Not the divorce. The list of things I can't talk to

you about," I say. Because that's the important thing about a best friend, I realize suddenly—the way you can talk honestly to her about whatever is bothering you. Not how much alike you are and how you agree on every little thing. And I'd rather know it now if Susanna can't be that kind of friend for me.

Hey, maybe I am finally growing up—a little.

Lacey will be so relieved. Hooray.

Susanna lets her breath out in a slow trickle of air. Her dirty hand reaches out, and she just barely touches my finger.

"Because I am kind of sad about Lacey moving out," I continue.

Susanna nods, silent.

"And I don't feel as bad as you probably think I should about my parents splitting up," I confess.

"I know," Susanna whispers. She grins a little. "The truth is, I don't care much about Lacey or your parents," she tells me. "I just don't want you to move away."

I turn to face Susanna. "You don't care about the divorce?" I say, amazed.

"Not really. Are you mad at me?" She waits for an answer.

"Nuh-uh," I reply after a moment. Wow—I was just worrying about telling *her* stuff, and it turns out *she* had something to say to *me!* "Let's promise we'll always be like this, OK?" I ask Susanna. "Compost fighters?"

Susanna frowns, thinking. Her face is pink with concentration. "Well, but we weren't really fighting this time," she objects.

"But if we ever do," I say.

Susanna grins. "Coffee grounds? Grass clippings? Rabbit poop?" she recites, as if imagining herself throwing all of those things right in my face.

"You know what I mean," I tell her, but I can't help smiling.

Susanna holds out her hand. "It's a deal," she says, and we shake hands.

Now, if it were only that easy with sisters.

9

WEEKEND FUN

I KNOW MY FATHER'S NEW PHONE NUMBER by heart now.

I figured that I might as well learn it, because it looks as if my parents are officially going through with the divorce.

We even have a schedule for weekends, and Lacey and I both hate it.

Here's how it's supposed to go: Every month, Lacey and I each have to spend one weekend alone with Mom and one weekend alone with Dad. Then I get to spend a weekend with Lacey at Dad's, and then Lacey comes over here and stays with Mom and me the next weekend.

It has been almost five weeks since that terrible night at the restaurant, and I've tried each kind of weekend once.

The best kind is when I'm alone with Mom, because Nibby is here, and I can always go hang out at Susanna's house if I get bored.

Next best is when I'm alone with Dad, because we do lots of fun stuff. Also, he lets me talk on the phone with Susanna for as long as I want.

Third best, or second worst, is when Lacey comes back to our house. Now that I'm used to having the bedroom all to myself, it's hard to share. And she tries to boss me around the minute she walks through the front door. But at least I can go outside to play with Nibby if my sister—my ex-sister—gets on my nerves too much.

If Mom isn't around, Lacey eventually starts to tease. She scratches herself and sings that stupid song, "Poison Ivy, Poison Ivy!" Then she inspects the bedroom—with a microscope, practically—to see if I've touched her stuff or moved anything even one inch.

"You can't boss me around," I told her last time, when she accused me of snooping in her part of the closet. "We've officially split! That means you don't get to be in charge of me anymore. Mom and Dad may make us still spend weekends together, but I don't have to listen to you."

"And I don't have to listen to you, either, Ivy. So stop talking."

But I admit it—I'm scared to touch her stuff.

And what does it really mean, divorcing your sister? I haven't quite figured that out yet. It would be pretty cool if she had to pay me alimony, half of her allowance, say, but I can't see that happening. And what if she decided she wanted joint custody of Nibby? Even though he's mine, and she doesn't really even like him? She says it's babyish for me to talk to Nibby as much as I do, but I don't care.

Maybe divorcing Lacey just means I should stop expecting anything from her. And I should definitely stop waiting for her to like me again.

It's her problem if she doesn't.

The worst weekend of the month is when I have to go over to Dad's when Lacey is staying there, too. None of my stuff is over there, and I miss Nibby and Susanna.

Also, Lacey and I had to share the dreaded futon last time.

Right before we went to bed, Lacey warned me that if I crossed over even one inch onto her half of the futon, she was going to pour ice water on my head. So I told her that if any part of her body touched my half of the futon, I was going to draw on her with permanent markers.

I would have done it, too! Big freckles, maybe, or hairy eyebrows, or a little black beard.

And that was before the tug-of-war over the blankets. We were like a TV show with the sound turned off, because we didn't want Dad to hear us fighting.

So that's what our weekends are like.

This whole new arrangement stinks, in my opinion. For example, I never seem to have exactly what I want when I am at my dad's. I usually need extra underpants or T-shirts. And even when I'm home with my mom, there's always something I left at Dad's that I need—like my library book, for instance. I had to pay a gigantic fine last week.

And this is going to be another one of those terrible weekends at Dad's. With Lacey.

"What are you looking for, Ivy?" Mom asks me.

I back out of the closet on my hands and knees. "My sleeping bag," I say. "I am not sleeping in the same bed as Lacey one more time, even if it is really a futon."

Mom laughs. She's laughing a lot more lately. I can tell that she is looking forward to having another weekend all by herself, and that makes me feel— really mad.

Or mad and sad at the same time.

"It's not that funny," I mutter.

"I think your sleeping bag is in the basement," Mom says, ignoring my bad mood. "But be sure and shake it out before you use it, in case of black widow spiders."

Black widow spiders. That's all I need.

I can feel the pile of hiking shoes, rain boots, and umbrellas move as I push the closet door shut. "What if I have to come home for something this weekend? Will you be here?" I ask, trying to keep the whine out of my voice.

"In and out," Mom says, fluffing her hair away from her neck. "I might be doing something with some of the girls."

"The girls" are my mother's new friends she met at job training. Everyone else in the world says women-this and women-that, but the ladies at job training decided to call themselves girls. Just to be different, I guess.

I scowl. "Well, but what if I need you?"

Mom laughs again and pulls me in for a hug. "You can always call and leave a message, Ivy. But I'm sure that your father can handle anything that comes up."

Your father. That's what she calls him now. "But what about Nibby?" I ask. "You won't forget to feed Nibby, will you? Even though you hate him?"

"Honey, I don't hate Nibby," my mom objects.

"And no," she adds, "I won't forget to feed him. Now hurry up with that sleeping bag, before your father gets here."

And good old Dad will be on time, for once, I think sourly, stomping down the basement stairs. Good old cheerful Dad, because he's been in a better mood lately, too, just like Mom.

Susanna says that my parents' good mood is probably only temporary, like that happy way you feel when you first go away on vacation—before you get homesick.

When do *I* get to be in a good mood? There's a little black cloud in my head that just won't go away.

Alone in the bedroom, I bend over and brush my hair hard, the way Lacey used to do when she lived here. She says that it helps make your hair shiny, but all it does is make me feel dizzy. Dizzy and stupid, because it's dumb to have to go to so much trouble just to go see your own father. Not to mention your ex-sister.

I flip my hair back and stare at myself in the mirror. Do I look any different? No, just pinker from being upside down for the last three minutes. And, of course, my hair is sticking out more. But, apart from that, it looks just about the same.

Frizzy and mud-colored, like my eyes.

Mom wishes my hair was long enough for me to pull back into a nice, neat ponytail, and I wish it was short, because it's summer. I would also like to have bangs, but oh, no. Mom says bangs would be a disaster with my kind of hair.

I bet I could make them work. There is such a thing as gel, isn't there?

Right now, my hair stops somewhere in the middle of my neck—where nobody likes it. I think it is stuck there. It's sure not growing very fast.

As I said before, the rest of me is still like a little kid, basically. I'm short, and my body is straight, just like my eyebrows. And like Susanna's body. But not like Lacey's body. Lacey has so many fancy bras that you would think she was a movie star or something. Big deal.

All those bras, and she still has only two you-know-whats. Which are not such big deals, if you know what I mean.

Lacey has been making fun of me and Susanna for that, too—how flat we are. But Susanna and I secretly think it's kind of gross the way girls' bodies change. We're glad that we're still skinny and small.

I look at the clock. It is already five-thirty. I'd better hurry up and get dressed for my weekend fun with Dad and Lacey!

"Your ride's here," Mom shouts up the stairs. *Your father, your ride.*

Oh well, at least things aren't as bad as they are at Karl Henniger's house. It sounds like a depressing TV movie over there. He even brags about it, how his mom and dad won't even look at one another. When his dad comes to pick him up for the weekend, he calls Karl's house on his cell phone—from the driveway! Just to say he's there.

And Karl says his mother always grabs for the phone and asks, "Who is this, please?" As if she didn't know.

"Hi, Dad," I say, coming into the hall. He already has my little red duffel bag hoisted over one shoulder. He's ready to go.

"Hi, toots," he says. "What's all this?" he asks, pointing at the sleeping bag I left by the front door.

"Lacey and I got kind of crowded last time we had to sleep together," I tell him.

"It's a big futon," he says, frowning a little as if he feels he ought to defend it.

"The girls can work this out, I think," Mom says in her cheerful voice—the one that is really saying, *Hey, this is kind of boring. Speed it up, would you?*

Her new voice.

"You're right," Dad agrees. "Come on, Ivy."

I have an empty feeling somewhere just above my stomach, and I try to think of a way to fill myself up. Hugging my rabbit might help. "Can't I just say good-bye to Nibby before we go? I'll bring him a piece of banana."

"I'll give Nibby some banana," Mom says.

"Lacey's waiting for us back at the apartment," Dad says. "Let's scoot—dinner will be ready soon."

"What are we having?" I ask him.

"Chicken."

"Mmmm, chicken," Mom says, shooing us out the door.

She sounds as though we are already gone.

10
WRECKED RICE

"**Y**UM. THIS TASTES A LITTLE BIT LIKE rabbit," Lacey remarks, smacking her lips over the chicken on her plate. Dad is standing at the stove stirring a pot of rice, and he doesn't hear what she says.

"Shut up," I tell Lacey—also quietly.

Lacey shrugs. "I was only saying . . ." she remarks. Then she starts singing under her breath. "Here comes Peter Cottontail, hopping down the bunny trail!" and her fork makes little hopping movements toward her big, lip-glossy mouth.

"Shut up," I say again, not so quietly this time.

"Girls," Dad warns, turning around. Then he asks, "Does anyone know how to make rice less soupy?"

"Turn up the heat?" Lacey suggests.

"The box said to cook it twenty minutes on low," Dad mumbles. But he turns the flame a little higher and stirs harder.

Lacey takes another bite of chicken, chews it thoughtfully, then swallows. She takes a dainty sip of milk, then clears her throat. "People do eat rabbits, you know," she informs me in a low voice.

"Not in America," I shoot back. "Anyway, that's just disgusting."

"No, rabbits are supposed to be very tender and delicious," Lacey says. "If they're young enough, that is, and if you cook them slowly enough. It says so in Dad's new cookbook. Which is American."

"You liar," I say. I put my fork down, though, because suddenly this chicken doesn't taste as good as it did a minute ago.

"Tender and delicious," Lacey repeats, as if quoting directly from the cookbook. She lifts another forkful of meat to her mouth.

"You're sick," I tell her.

"Hmm," she says softly, as though she is thinking aloud, "I wonder if Mom remembered to feed Nibby. We wouldn't want him to get too—skinny!" Right after she says the word "skinny," she snaps the meat off her fork like a crocodile during feeding time at the zoo.

"Shut up."

"I'll bet she forgot to feed him," Lacey says, shaking her head sadly. "Probably Nibby is wondering where his dinner is, right about now. And his water, too, which would be a whole lot worse—because if an animal runs out of water in the summer, he really, really suffers."

"Shut up," I yell, and I pick up my glass of milk and throw it—right in her face!

Which I have never done before.

It feels kind of good to do this, but only for a second.

"Ivy!" Lacey screeches.

My dad turns around, spoon in the air, with big gobs of sticky rice falling from it. That rice does not look right to me. "What in the Sam Hill is going on?" he asks—which is what he says to us when he's extremely mad. "Sam Hill" is a more polite way of saying "hell," I think.

"She sploshed me," Lacey squeals, outraged. She is mopping her face with a napkin by now, but it's not doing much good. Strands of dripping blond hair are hanging in her face, and there are dark patches all across the top of her shirt. There is even milk on Dad's new tablecloth, the one he bought to show Lacey and me that this is his permanent home, not just a temporary place to stay.

As if we hadn't figured that out already.

"Ivy?" Dad asks, turning to me.

The empty glass of milk is still in my hand.

"It—it slipped?" I say, trying out the words.

"You liar," Lacey screams.

"You're the liar," I yell back. "You told me that Americans eat rabbits!"

"They do!"

Another lump of rice falls to the floor. I think that Dad is paralyzed or something. "Uh," he finally says, "I guess some Americans eat some rabbits." Then he turns to me. "But not pets," he says. There is a pleading look in his eyes.

"Told you," Lacey says, triumphant. "Rabbits are supposed to be nice and tender, aren't they, Dad?"

"That's enough, Lacey," Dad says, seeing the look on my face.

"That's enough?" Lacey says, clearly not believing her ears. "When Ivy threw her whole glass of milk right in my face?"

"It wasn't a whole glass of milk," I interrupt. "I already drank some of it."

Lacey springs up from her chair. "Well, I'm taking a shower—if it's all right with you," she says to Dad in her most sarcastic voice.

"Fine with me," Dad says. He sighs and holds his empty hand up in pretend surrender.

"It's fine with me, too," I chime in. "In fact, I was going to suggest it."

But my words are the last straw for Lacey. She whirls toward me and mutters, "Everything was great here, until you came along. So are you going to ruin things at Dad's, too?"

What in the world is she talking about? I might have ruined things by accident for Lacey when I was a baby, but I couldn't help being born. And now, well, I'm only here because Mom and Dad are making me be here. Obviously, I'd rather be someplace else.

I can't believe I used to like Lacey. Love her, even.

"Yeah," I say. "I'm going to ruin everything, everywhere I go. That's my big plan."

"Well, congratulations, you succeeded!" Lacey yells, and she runs into the bathroom crying.

Dad and I look at each other for about a hundred years, it seems. I clasp my hands together underneath the table. Maybe that will stop them from shaking.

Finally, Dad jams the spoon back into the pot of wrecked rice and says, "If I'd had my wits about me, I'd have ordered out. Some Chinese food, maybe, or a nice pizza."

11

BANGS

MY DAD IS IN THE APARTMENT BASEMENT stuffing his precious new tablecloth and napkins into the coin-operated washing machine, and I am in the bathroom cutting bangs in my hair.

Only it's harder than I thought it would be.

Lacey is pounding on the locked door. "Hurry up," she yells—through the keyhole, practically. "I have to go!"

"I'm hurrying," I drawl. I tilt my head and look at my brand-new bangs. The mirror is still steamy from Lacey's hour-long stay in the bathroom. She hogged the room while she was taking her shower and giving herself a manicure, so why shouldn't I have a turn?

And I don't believe that she really has to go.

My bangs look slanted. I try bending my head in the other direction to even them up, but that only makes my neck feel funny. Now I look like a person with weird bangs—and a sore neck.

I straighten up and try hacking off a more even line of hair with Dad's little manicure scissors. I press my new bangs flat as I cut. When I let go, though, the hair springs up crooked again. Crooked—and even shorter.

My bangs are sticking straight out, practically.

I have always wanted bangs, though. And if Dad's doing what he wants, living in this terrible apartment, and Mom's doing what she wants, going out with the old-lady "girls," and Lacey's doing what she wants, driving me crazy, why shouldn't I do something I want to do?

Maybe the bangs just aren't wide enough. I try to think about it calmly, squinting through hot tears. I take a breath, hold it, and cut off a hunk of side hair. I toss it into the toilet.

There is so much hair in the toilet already that it almost looks as though somebody tried to drown a wig. A wig made of frizzy mud-brown hair.

It gives me a funny feeling, seeing all that hair. I flush, and then I flush again.

And again.

"What are you doing in there?" Lacey squawks through the door. "Are you sick or something? Because I'm not taking care of you if you're sick." She pounds on the door—using her fist this time.

I know Lacey doesn't want to take care of me. She doesn't have to keep saying it!

I blow my nose. I try to wipe leftover hair out of the sink with a handful of Kleenexes, and I flush one more time. The toilet is making a funny noise now, and hair and baby-blue Kleenexes are swirling around in a lazy circle.

"I'm telling," Lacey yells, which is dumb, because what is there to tell? For all she knows, I have food poisoning from terrible chicken and gloppy rice, which miraculously turned out burned and crunchy-raw at the same time.

She doesn't know what I've really been doing.
Yet.

I decide to unlock the bathroom door. After all, it's my hair. I should be able to cut it if I want. And I hate to say so, but I can't hide in here forever.

Lacey takes a step back when she sees me, her eyes wide. And then she cracks up. "I don't believe it," she says, almost gasping for air. She clutches at herself, and her green-polished fingernails gleam.

"Shut up! What are you laughing at?" I say, trying to cover my hair with my hands.

"Your bangs," Lacey squeals. "What are you going to do, walk around with your hands on your forehead for the rest of your life?"

I make myself lower my hands. And I can feel my sawed-off bangs bounce up. *Boi-i-ing!*

"Ah-h-h," Lacey says, laughing harder. She's on the floor by now. Behind me, the toilet is still gurgling. It sounds as though it's strangling on my hair, which by now I am wishing was stuck back on my head, where it belongs.

"Shut up," I say again.

"Make me," she says.

But she's saying it to the wrong person on the wrong day—because I would absolutely love to make Lacey shut up.

I give her a little kick. "Lacey, Lacey, ugly facey," I chant.

Lacey socks me in the leg, not very hard. "At least Mom and Dad didn't name me after a weed," she says from the floor. "They probably didn't even want you," she adds.

I kick again, harder. "Ivy's not a weed," I say. "It's a plant. A very expensive plant."

"It is not," she says. "It's a weed, practically. And it climbs all over the nice plants in the garden, and they hate it. I looked it up."

That's it for me, and I pounce on her.

"Yah-h-h-h!" Lacey screams, and she starts hitting me with her fists—the same way she pounded on the bathroom door.

Which is probably what made me cut my bangs too short.

So I pound her, too.

And then it's as if I am stepping back and watching myself: My sister is rolling around on the floor, and so am I. It seems as though it must be someone else, not me, who is slugging her sister and trying to pull her sister's perfect blond hair out in chunks.

And I almost can't feel Lacey twisting, pinching, and gouging me. *Almost.*

Ow! Look at that, she's even trying to bite me!

We are actually having a fight.

We've yelled at each other before, and shoved each other, too—but not flat-out whomped each other.

And it's weird, but on top of everything else, it feels as though we're getting wet!

"Quit it," I scream, trying to shove her rattlesnake mouth away from my arm. "I'll scratch your ugly blond face, I swear I will. I'll punch you in the nose," I warn her, extra-loud. I make my hand into a fist, ready to attack.

"You're the ugly one. Everybody says so!" Lacey screeches as we thrash around on the floor. "The only one who can stand you is that stupid rabbit. Let's see how he likes you with a black eye!"

We roll back and forth in Dad's tiny hall. And it feels as if we're covered with hair.

"Nibby is not stupid!" I shriek, and I try to punch Lacey in the nose, but she jerks my hand away.

No, wait—someone else is twisting my fist away from my sister's horrible face.

It's Dad!

"What in the Sam Hill is going on?" he bellows.

Lacey is coughing, the big faker, like I've been choking her or something. She's on her hands and knees in the . . . mess. Because the toilet has over-flowed, and there is water, hair, and shreds of blue Kleenex all over the bathroom floor. And the whole thing has washed out into the hall.

We've been rolling around in toilet water.

My heart is pounding, and I feel as if I'm about to throw up.

"This is disgusting," Lacey wails. "And—look!" she adds, holding out a trembling hand.

Oh no, one of her poor fingernails is broken.

Now I really feel bad.

12

SISTER SPLIT

WELL, HERE WE ARE, ALL TOGETHER AGAIN—
Mom and Dad and Lacey and me, just like one big, happy family. It is nine o'clock at night, and I am sitting at one end of Dad's sofa bed, sticky and miserable. Lacey is sitting at the other end.

She might be miserable, too, only I don't care.

Dad is standing in front of us, arms folded, and so is my mom, who has appeared out of nowhere. Dad must have called her up and told her this was an emergency.

I have finally stopped shaking from the fight, but now I am shivering from being wet and hairy. I wish they would just let us take showers and go to sleep.

But oh, no. We have to talk.

"So, what are we going to do about you two?" Dad asks.

"Fighting," Mom mutters under her breath. She actually sounds shocked.

I stop shivering. Suddenly, I am flooded with anger so hot that it makes me dizzy, and I jump to my feet. "Well, what did you expect?" I ask them. "I already told you guys I wanted a divorce from Lacey, didn't I? So why do you keep throwing us together? No one's making *you* spend every other weekend with each other, are they?"

Mom and Dad and Lacey blink at me like startled owls, but Lacey recovers first.

"Yeah," she says, turning to face our parents. "How come you two don't have to live together, but we do?"

"This—this isn't about us," my dad says, but he sounds a little uncertain.

I actually stomp my foot. "You are not taking me seriously!" I shout.

Lacey stares at me. Mom and Dad just look at each other.

I try again. "You guys are getting divorced, aren't you? Well, this is a sister split."

Dad shakes his head. "There's a big difference between what your mom and I are doing and 'a sister split,' as you call it," he says. "Marriage is a legal contract, for one thing, and we have decided—after a lot of painful soul-searching, let me assure you—to end that contract."

"You still haven't given us one good reason why!" Lacey challenges him.

Mom exchanges a lightning-quick glance with Dad. "This is not something that parents have to explain to their children," she says. "It's our decision, and our decision alone."

"Marriage is the only family relationship that can be legally ended," Dad continues, before Lacey or I can take over the conversation again. "But you two are going to be sisters forever, just the way we'll be your parents forever."

"I'll split up with her illegally, then," I say, stubborn. "And this isn't something I have to explain to *you.* But from now on, no more sharing bags of M&M's with Lacey. No more watching TV together in our pajamas. No more talking in the dark. It's over!"

Lacey stares down at her hands. She's probably worried about those imaginary M&M's.

"Nice try, Ivy," my father finally rumbles, "but don't change the subject, which is the fact that you two were trying to hurt each other tonight. Rolling around like alley cats. I never saw such a thing!"

"I can't believe it," my mother says, shaking her head.

Lacey wriggles impatiently on the sofa. "Why?" she asks. "Why can't you believe that Ivy and I hate each other? You guys hate each other. Maybe our whole family is just . . . messed up, that's all."

"We are not 'messed up,' as you put it," my dad objects.

"Lots of people have problems," Mom says, her voice shaking a little.

"Problems?" Lacey shouts, jumping to her feet. "My mother and father are getting a divorce, my own sister attacked me, I've got a broken fingernail, and I'm all covered with Ivy's revolting hair! That's not 'having problems.' That's messed up!"

"Lacey, keep your voice down," Dad says, looking around, as though we might be bothering his new neighbors.

Which we probably are, but who cares? We could make a special card to send them, like the one Mom and Dad sent out at Christmas—before I was born. *Happy weekend from the Millers!*

"You cannot make us like each other," I say, crossing my arms. "What are you going to do, lock us in a room together until we come out hugging?"

Mom and Dad look at each other again. "You know, that's not such a terrible idea," Dad says.

"Oh, great," Lacey mumbles. "Thanks a lot, Ivy. You've done it again."

"I wasn't serious. And it's a *terrible* idea!" I tell her. What a dumb thing to have to explain. Typical Lacey.

"Well, *I'm* serious," Mom says, turning to Dad. "What about it?"

"No fair," Lacey shouts. "Nobody locked you guys in a room together until you came out hugging and everything."

"Well, maybe somebody should have—before it was too late," Dad says, and my mom bites her lips together and looks down at the floor.

"Now look what you did," I tell Lacey.

"You're the one who did it, you—you—"

"Shut up!"

"No, both of you shut up," Dad tells us.

I think that it is the first time he has ever said that to us.

"I'm sick of this garbage," he continues. "You two can just sit here and cool your fannies while your mother and I go in the other room to discuss this. And let me know if the doorbell rings." Because Dad has called an all-night plumber to come over and fix his toilet.

Which will probably cost about a hundred dollars an hour, and I'll never hear the end of it.

Lacey flumps back onto the sofa, and my parents walk into the kitchen. It is only a few steps away, but they are whispering, so we can't hear them.

About a million years go by.

"OK," Dad says, finally walking back into the room with Mom. "Here's the deal . . ."

13

SATURDAY MORNING

I **WAKE UP IN MY MOM AND DAD'S BED, THE ONE** they used to share when they were living together.

Before Dad started sleeping on the sofa.

I don't even have to open my eyes to know where I am. A part of me can still remember lying here between my parents, cuddling, a long, long time ago. Sometimes Lacey was with us, too.

I also don't have to open my eyes to know that Lacey is here next to me. I can smell her. She uses this shampoo that smells like some weird kind of fruit punch that has sat around too long.

Yes, she managed to drag some of her toiletries home with her last night. Lacey might forget to do her math homework for three weeks straight, like she did last spring, but she's not the type of girl who's ever going to forget her shampoo and conditioner.

"I know you're awake," Lacey whispers.

"So what?" I say, my eyes still shut. "I know you're awake, too."

"This is all your fault," Lacey says in her normal voice.

I can't really argue with her about that—but then, I never actually expected that Mom and Dad would go through with this.

We are locked in their bedroom—their old bedroom, that is—for the entire weekend. They would not even let us stay in our own room, because there's no bathroom attached.

The curtains are pulled tightly shut. I am tucked between faded blue paisley sheets, and Mom and Dad's cotton blanket has slithered onto the floor, as if trying to get away.

"So what if it's my fault?" I say to Lacey.

There is a knock on the door, but it's more of an *I'm-coming-in!* knock than a *May-I-come-in?* one. Lacey flings herself back onto the bed to pretend that she is asleep just as the door opens. She is wearing a frayed navy blue T-shirt and baggy plaid pajama bottoms.

It's a look, she says.

I pretend I'm asleep, too, but I peek a little and see Mom carry a tray to her dressing table. She puts it down and leaves the room, clicking the door shut behind her.

Breakfast.

My mouth starts watering—I can't help it.

Lacey lifts up her head. "French toast," she says in a sneering voice. "Like that's going to make everything OK."

I am already halfway across the room to the dressing table. "I'll eat yours, if you hate it so much." My pink-and-white-striped nightgown sways around my ankles as I walk.

"You'd better not," she warns, springing up from the bed.

We carry our full plates back to bed and sit cross-legged in the gloom, munching away. I try to eat slowly, because after this, there will be no more excitement until lunchtime. Only I can't eat slowly. Fighting makes me hungry, I guess.

"We should call the police," Lacey says, chewing.

"And tell them what?" I ask her. "That our mom just brought us French toast on a golden tray?"

I try not to look at the black-and-blue mark I left on her arm last night. Well, she probably left marks on me, too, hitting me with all those rings on.

"And anyway," I point out, "they took the phone

away. We can't even call our friends, much less the police."

They also carried out the TV set and the clock radio, so we'd have to communicate with each other for a change, Mom said.

"We could scream for Mrs. Pincus to come help us," Lacey suggests, pointing her fork toward the window.

"Sure," I say, thinking of how hard it is to get Mrs. Pincus's attention even when you are standing right in front of her. *You're right on the astrological cusp,* she'd probably say, her eyes wide. *That makes all the difference, you know.* "Or you could just climb out the window and down that tree, for that matter," I tell Lacey. "It's not like Mom and Dad would call the cops on you. Or you could just walk out the door."

She won't, I know. Oh, she tried to start a little revolution last night, when Mom and Dad laid out the details of their plan. "You can't make me do this," she said, shaking her head. We were still at Dad's apartment then.

But Dad just laughed. "And you can't make us give you an allowance, or buy you those new clothes for school you've been begging for, or let you stay out late with your friends on the weekend, or allow you to get your driver's license next year, or—"

"You're threatening me!" Lacey had bellowed, but she backed right down.

So, there were three rules we were given: no leaving until given permission, no hiding in the bathroom or the closet, and no hitting.

That last rule is a relief, anyway.

"I could be enjoying myself at Dad's right now," Lacey grumbles, shooting me a dirty look. "I'd still be asleep." She runs a finger through the leftover syrup on her plate and licks it clean.

If I did that, she'd tell me how gross I was.

"Well," I say, "I could be over at Susanna's or out in the backyard playing with Nibby," I tell Lacey. "I have stuff to do, too, you know." I feel a pang when I say Nibby's name, because—is Mom really taking good enough care of him?

"I meant to talk to you about that rabbit," Lacey says in a casual voice.

Uh-oh. I can feel my right hand start to curl into a fist again. "What about him?" I ask.

She shrugs. "It's just that it's kind of lame, playing with a pet all the time, isn't it? At your age? I think it's embarrassing, actually."

"I like him," I hear myself telling my sister. *And he likes me!* is what I don't say.

"Stop playing with your hair," Lacey snaps, looking at me sideways.

I take my hand down from my bristly bangs. "I wasn't," I tell her.

Lacey shakes her head, looking sad. "You're going to have to stay inside for the rest of the summer until your hair looks normal again. Too bad. Or—or you could wear a big hat all the time. That would look nice," she adds sarcastically.

"Oh, give it a rest," I tell her. "You're just trying to start another fight, that's all."

"Well, why shouldn't I?" she asks. "I'm bored, and there's nothing else to do. This is going to be a long weekend."

"The longest," I say, agreeing with her—for once. "And stay on your side of the bed while you're at it."

"I am on my side of the bed."

"No, you're not," I tell her, and I pull the covers smooth and draw my finger down the middle of the bed. "You stay on that side of the imaginary line, and I'll stay on this side."

"This is so lame," Lacey says, and she flops down on her back, flinging one arm over onto my side of the bed. On purpose! She shuts her eyes as if she is dying of boredom.

"Wait, then—I'll make it a real line," I tell her.

I know that my mother keeps a roll of masking tape in the top drawer of her desk, and now is the time to use it.

"What are you doing?" Lacey asks a moment later, eyes still squinched shut.

"Dividing things up," I say, and the tape makes a whirring noise as I pull it across the pillows, down the still-warm sheets, and across Lacey's arm.

She jumps up, ruining my nice, neat line of tape. "What are you doing?" she asks again, as if I have finally gone nuts. She wads up the sticky tape.

"I already told you." I start in on the floor. "You stay on that side of the bed and you'll be OK."

"Why?" Lacey says. "What are you going to do if I cross over the magic line? Scare me to death with your bangs?"

I resist the urge to touch my hair again. Instead, I yank some more tape from the roll. "So, are you going to move," I ask my sister, "or should I just tape right over you?"

14

LO-O-O-ONG HOURS

DAD'S ON DUTY NOW, APPARENTLY. HE DOESN'T mention the tape—which, by the time he brings us lunch, crisscrosses much of the room. And the bathroom. I even tried dividing the toilet in half, but that didn't work.

Dad doesn't seem to care that there is tape all over everything. In fact, he looks as though he is trying not to laugh.

He's got a lot of nerve! We just ignore him. He whisks the curtains open, and the bedroom fills with stripes of noonday light.

"Look," I say to Lacey after a silent lunch of grilled cheese sandwiches, celery sticks, and butterscotch pudding cups. "We have to come up with a way to get out of here."

Lacey nods, even though I can tell she doesn't like agreeing with me.

"Maybe we can trick them into thinking we've made up," I say.

"Them," Lacey echoes gloomily. "Mom and Dad, Sylvia and Frank. This girl I know calls her parents by their first names." Lacey stares lazily up at the ceiling and picks at what is left of her green fingernail polish. "Can you imagine Mom and Dad letting us call them Sylvia and Frank?"

"We could call them by their last names," I suggest. "Mr. and Mrs. Miller," I say, trying it out.

Lacey laughs. "Yeah, right."

"Or we could just call them *Them*," I continue. It's kind of fun making her laugh.

"*Us* versus *Them*," Lacey says.

"That doesn't sound right," I tell her.

"Well, yeah," she says, "because in our family, *Us* is me and Dad now, and *Them* is you and Mom."

"I think it's the other way around," I object. "Mom and I are *Us*."

Lacey sighs. "Whatever. I'm just saying in other families, *Us* is the kids and *Them* is the parents."

"Oh," I say. I think about that for awhile.

But we're not other families, so it's hard.

"I do kind of like your idea about calling them Mr. and Mrs. Miller, though," Lacey tells me.

"I am really, really glad that I got this side of the room," Lacey tells me a couple lo-o-o-ong hours later. She is lying on the floor near the door like a giant X, rings glimmering in a shaft of sunlight. She works her finger through a hole in her T-shirt, making the hole bigger.

The stripes of light are lower on the flowered wall now, but the bedroom still smells like a mixture of maple syrup and grilled cheese. This is kind of like living in a diner, I think lazily, or like being in jail. Maybe I should make a little mark on the windowsill to show that one day has almost gone by.

"How come you like that side of the room?" I ask from where I am lying.

I'm on the little striped area rug, and I can see straight out the window from this angle. It's very interesting out there—I even saw a squirrel about fifteen minutes ago. I think he was holding a nut. Or maybe it was a little brown suitcase.

I'd rather have a window than a door any day, especially when we're not allowed to use the door.

I changed into shorts and a T-shirt an hour ago, just for something to do, but Lacey is still in her so-called pajamas, although she is getting ready to do her nails again. She already washed her face and put on makeup. Lacey would probably wear makeup on an expedition to Antarctica.

I try to imagine her taking just such a trip. Bon voyage!

"Well," Lacey explains, sounding logical as she douses a cotton pad with polish remover, "Mrs. Miller is probably downstairs right now, right? Or maybe she's even gone out. So, if a bad guy decides that he wants to break into this house, he'll probably shinny up that tree out there and climb right in through the window. He'll get you first—and I'll have time to escape."

Yikes!

I want to jump up and lock myself in the bathroom, but I force myself to hold still. Anyway, there's no lock on the bathroom door.

"Oh, yeah?" I say, trying to sound bored. "I think it's more likely that the bad guy will probably just sneak up the stairs, because I'll bet Mr. Miller is long gone by now, and Mrs. Miller is taking a nap on the sofa. She won't even hear the bad guy come in. And so he'll o-o-o-open the bedroom door—and get you first. But I'll have time to escape out the window! Thanks, by the way."

"Give it up, Ivy," Lacey says smugly. "You're the chicken in this family." She wipes the soaked cotton pad on each of her nails, removing the last of the green polish, and the stink from the polish remover fills the room.

I could complain about it, of course, but that would only make her happy. So instead, I just pray for her to spill the remover all over Mom's floor. Then Lacey will really be in trouble!

Please, please.

But no such luck.

And Lacey calling me chicken is the last I hear from her for two whole hours. Boo hoo hoo.

However, one good thing about the silent treatment is that it gives you time to think.

Or to take a nap . . .

15

"Everybody loves Saturday Night!"

It's my mother's turn again, I guess.
"Saturday night," she announces as if it's news. She's just entered the room backward, carrying our dinner tray. "Everybody loves Saturday night!" she sings.

Lacey sits up in bed, looking offended. "Mother, that's just cruel," she says. Mascara smudges under her eyes make her look like some weird kind of cat.

I want to back Lacey up on this one, but my brain feels muzzy from conking out in the middle of the afternoon. I guess that's what happens when your poor body is in shock from getting a bad haircut, fighting in toilet water, and having to share a bed with a sister who hates you.

My mouth feels as though there's a sock in it—an old gym sock, maybe, or a couple of those curly, flesh-colored things they make you wear in shoe stores to try stuff on, if you're not wearing socks of your own. "Muh," I say, scowling.

Mom just laughs some more. Then she sits down on the unmade bed and announces, "Your father and I have decided to help you girls make up."

Sparks practically fly from Lacey's head, she's so mad. "Oh, great, so now you guys decide to be a team and agree on everything? After you've already ruined our lives?"

Mom looks surprised, and she tries to calm Lacey down. "Honey, I hardly think that giving you girls a time out—even for a whole weekend—qualifies as ruining your lives."

"I'm not talking about that, Mother," Lacey says, looking totally exasperated.

"Well, what are you talking about?" Mom asks.

Lacey jumps up and begins to shout. "I'm talking about you and Dad deciding to split up just when I'm finally starting high school—which, if you even bothered to think about it for one single second, you'd realize I've been looking forward to my whole life long. Thanks a lot!"

High school? What does my parents' divorce have to do with Lacey going to high school? I don't get it.

Mom doesn't get it, either. "What in the world are you talking about, Lacey?"

"I'm talking about how you and Dad want to just do your own thing," Lacey sputters, quoting one of Dad's favorite sayings from the sixties, "when it's finally my turn to have a little fun. You're just going to dump Ivy on me while you guys go out and start over like a couple of kids!"

Whoa. Hold on a minute. "Dump me?" I squawk, but my mother isn't listening.

"Lacey, is that why you moved out?" she is asking my sister.

"It's one of the reasons," Lacey says, lifting up her chin.

"I don't need you to baby-sit me, you jerk," I tell Lacey. This is not exactly the truth, but I'm not going to let her blame everything on me! "Mrs. Pincus would help out if something went wrong," I say.

"Yeah, right, Ivy," Lacey says. "If you broke your leg, she'd tell you that you were just experiencing some bad karma."

My mother is shaking her head as though she is trying to rearrange the thoughts inside.

"Mom, wake up and smell the latte!" Lacey says to her. "I'm fifteen years old! Why would I want to be stuck with Ivy all the time? She's eleven! We can't be friends anymore."

I would argue with her, but I have to admit that she's right. Still, I am a little surprised to hear Lacey say those words. They hurt.

"I don't even want to be friends with you," I say. I don't mean it, not really, but I don't want to be friends with her if she doesn't want to be friends with me!

The bedroom door opens a crack. Dad pokes his head around the corner cautiously, as though he half expects a cartoon pie to hit him in the face. "Is it safe to come in?" he asks.

Mom gives him a grateful look. This is the first time in a long time that she's seemed honestly glad to see him. "Help me out here, Frank," she says, sounding desperate, and Dad sidles into the room.

So, here we all are again.

The room is silent for a moment. Specks of dust sift to the floor, through the last low stripes of evening light that slice sideways, and the tarnished brass clock on Mom's desk gives a couple of extra-loud ticks. That clock sounds almost as nervous as my dad.

"Lacey was just saying that you guys are wrecking her whole life by dumping me on her all the time," I tell Dad.

"I didn't say that. Not exactly," Lacey protests. Her words sound a little feeble, but she shoots me a look that's so mean, it gives me the shivers. "In fact," she says, turning to Dad, "I love my adorable sister. Now are you happy? Now can I get out of here and go back to your apartment—where I belong?"

"Let her go," I say, but Lacey does not seem to appreciate this little show of support.

"Your father and I will decide where you 'belong,' Miss Lacey," Mom says in her that's-that tone of voice. "For now, that's right here, in this room. And what I've been trying to say is, we've decided to help you two girls patch things up by giving you a little assignment." She looks at Dad for support.

"Homework? In the summer?" I squawk.

"That's right," Dad says, taking over. "After you eat this nice dinner your mother has fixed, each of you is to make a list of three things that you like about your one-and-only sister."

"It will help pass the time," Mom says, as if trying to tempt us with something sweet.

"*Mo-ther,*" Lacey complains, rolling her eyes. "Next thing you know, you'll be putting me and Ivy on some revolting courtroom TV show, just so some whacked-out judge can yell at us in front of a live studio audience. You'd like that, wouldn't you?"

"Ivy and me," Mom corrects her, and Lacey throws a pillow—onto my side of the room.

"*Hey,*" I yell, and I point to the line of tape.

"Well, I can tell you three things I like about Ivy

right now!" Lacey says, jumping to her feet. Her plaid pajama bottoms sag, and she hoists them up with such a furious jerk that she jumps a little. "First, I'm glad there's only one of her. Second, I'm just thrilled that she lives here and not with Dad, so I don't have to stare at her stupid face every day anymore. And third, I can't wait to graduate and go off to college and never see her again!"

Our parents' jaws are practically hanging open in amazement by this time, but mine feels as though someone has turned a big old crank and shut it tight. I can't speak, I am so angry.

"Well, Lacey," Mom says sarcastically, "you've managed to make each of those three things on your list, which is supposedly about Ivy, really be about you. Congratulations."

Lacey blushes.

Hah!

"Now, your dinner's over on the dressing table," Mom continues coolly, "and there's notebook paper in the top drawer of my desk. You girls know the assignment."

And out she and Dad go, united at last.

16

A VERY HARD ASSIGNMENT

"**H**AVE YOU REALLY BEEN LOOKING FORWARD to high school your whole life long?" I ask after licking my fingers clean—because letting your table manners slide has to be one of the good things about being locked up for the weekend, doesn't it?

"Yeah," Lacey says, not looking up from the old magazine she has been thumbing through while she eats her chicken, baked potato, and peas. No dessert tonight, I guess.

"I definitely do not think this marriage can be saved," she adds, jabbing a finger at the article she has been reading. "In fact, I have never read one of these things where I think the marriage can be saved—which is one of the reasons I'm never getting married!" She looks at me as if she is expecting an argument.

"Well, me either," I say. "What if I accidentally married someone who didn't like rabbits?"

Lacey almost smiles. "That would be a complete tragedy," she says. She does not sound as though she means it, however.

"What's so great about high school?" I ask, banging my drumstick bone on the plate as if keeping time to special music Lacey can't hear.

"Oh, nothing—apart from getting to drive, and going shopping all by yourself or with your friends for a change, instead of with your mom or your little sister, and staying out late on the weekends, and meeting new guys," she says, flipping her hair back over her shoulder. "High school is going to be the highlight of my entire life, and I plan to enjoy every minute of it."

Not if you don't pass that summer school class, I feel like saying. But I don't.

"I'm going to try to get a boyfriend first thing," Lacey continues, as if she is outlining her plan to buy a new red sweater for fall. "I'll get invited to more parties that way. If I don't end up baby-sitting you all the time, that is." Lacey turns a magazine page angrily.

"You won't," I say, scowling. "I'll tell Mrs. Miller that I don't want you anywhere near me."

Lacey shrugs. "Well, I don't believe you. But it's not up to either one of us," she says gloomily. "When I go to college, I'm going *far* away. The farther, the better," she stresses.

I can't resist it. "Yeah," I tell her. "Maybe someone will offer you a math scholarship."

I brood over my list of three things I like about Lacey. I feel like doing exactly what she did and making it all about me.

I could say I like that she moved out, because I always wanted a room of my own. And that I'm glad when Lacey goes out with her friends, because then she's not around to make fun of Susanna and me. And last, I could write that I'm absolutely thrilled that Lacey wants to go far, far away to college, because then it will almost be like she was never born. And I will get to be an only child.

But I know deep down that writing a list like this will get me nowhere, fast.

The last daylight is gone now, and I turn on the bedside lamp with still-greasy fingers. A little puddle of golden light seems as though it is bravely trying to warm the chill that has grown between me and my sister. But it's not succeeding.

How will this end? Lacey will move back in with my dad, I guess, and eventually leave for college, and then I'll never see her again. Well, isn't that just what I wanted when I said we should get a divorce?

I look over at Lacey, who is still reading her magazine, or at least pretending to. "I'm bored out of my skull," she says, not looking up. "Why should we be the ones who get punished just because Mr. and Mrs. Miller messed up their marriage?"

"We're getting punished because we had a fight," I remind her.

"Yeah, but what's so bad about fighting?" she persists. "You fight with Susanna, don't you?"

Susanna. Now Lacey is going to start in on her, and that will be the end of me trying to be nice. "Let's keep Susanna out of this," I say, hoping that I sound as though I don't much care if Lacey does or does not take this advice. "She's my best friend, in case you forgot."

"How could I forget?" she asks me. "You and your little friend—and I do mean little—are always in my face. You guys look like a couple of Popsicle sticks, you're so skinny."

Well, no one will ever say that about you, I could say—and I know it would shut her right up. Because Lacey is not fat, true, but she has gotten a little pudgy lately. And she's worried about it, I know. She always checks out her stomach in the mirror, for example. *You'll never get a boyfriend,* I could tell her if I wanted to be really mean. *And you're going to be fat someday, too, just like Mom!*

But I don't say anything. Just because you *can* say something doesn't necessarily mean that you should.

I sure wish someone would tell Lacey that!

"When you and Susanna get together, you look like a couple of second-graders," Lacey continues. "With your knees all scuffed up! It's just pathetic."

"What do you care what we look like?" I ask. "At least we're not sticking out our boobies all the time."

"That's because you guys don't have boobies," Lacey says, smirking, and she smooths her hands across the front of her tight T-shirt. The same one she slept in, by the way.

"We don't even want any," I inform her.

"Liar. And you guys are so infantile, playing with those stupid rabbits every chance you get," Lacey sneers.

"What do you have against rabbits, anyway?" I ask. "That's kind of a weird hang-up, if you ask me."

Lacey slaps her magazine shut with a dramatic sigh and shoves it away with her foot. "Get a clue, why don't you—it's not really the rabbits," she says, frustrated. "Oh, just forget about it. You wouldn't understand what I mean."

Lacey gathers her blond hair behind her neck and glances around as if she is looking for a rubber band. Giving up, she lets her hair fall loose again across her shoulders.

I wish my hair did that. "*You* don't even know what you mean," I say, daring her to explain.

"I do too! I'm trying to tell you to grow up, for pete's sake. Just grow up."

"I'm plenty grown up," I protest, wondering secretly if that's true. Because would a grown-up person be as nervous as I am about her parents getting a divorce, or about burglars breaking into the house when she's home alone, or about something bad happening to her pet rabbit?

Or as nervous as I am about this one little fight with Lacey, my former big sister?

"You're not grown-up enough to make it through Mom and Dad's breakup without me there to hold your hand every step of the way," Lacey says. "I can see the handwriting on the wall."

Goosebumps crawl up each of my arms as I watch her blue eyes fill with tears, because Lacey hardly ever cries. I don't know where to look, in fact.

She flops back onto Mom's wrinkly pillow and covers her eyes with her hands. My buttery baked potato rolls off my dinner plate and onto the blanket and almost bumps into her leg.

"Want a Kleenex?" I ask her.

"No," she says, sounding disgusted with me for even asking. She rubs her arm, which, as I mentioned before, is bruised from last night's fight. "Look what you did," she says, holding it out for inspection.

"It was self-defense," I say. "You were just about to bite me, don't forget. And now you're giving me a headache."

"So what else is new?" Lacey says. "You were going to scratch my face last night! And you tried to pull my hair out, too."

"Well, that's what you get for being a garbage fighter," I tell her.

"A what?" Lacey replies, sitting up straight from the waist, like a zombie.

"A garbage fighter," I say, not backing down. And then I take a deep breath and tell her my new theory about compost fights, which can be good, as opposed to garbage fights, which are always bad. Because what do I have to lose?

Lacey shakes her head in wonderment. "You are out—of—your—mind," she says slowly.

"See? That's an example of garbage fighting," I snap at her.

"Oh, OK," she says, looking fake-concerned. "I really fe-e-e-el that you-u-u might be losing your ma-a-arbles," she enunciates slowly.

Just then, with perfect timing, my cold potato decides to take another hike and rolls against Lacey's bare foot. "Yah-h-h!" she squawks, and she picks up the potato as if it is swarming with nuclear waste and drops it onto my plate. "This place is a pigsty," she says, suddenly Miss Clean.

She's right, though. The blanket is heaped on the floor at the foot of the bed, and the sheets are practically in knots by now. Discarded magazines form a crazy quilt on the bed, and a circle of wadded-up tissues surrounds the wastebasket on Lacey's side of the room. Lingering smells from breakfast, lunch, and dinner hang in the air.

"You are such a slob, Ivy," my sister says, shaking her head.

I try not to laugh. "You're not even trying to fight fair," I say, and I start to doodle on my piece of notebook paper. I'm embarrassed I even attempted to explain my theory to her.

"Really, I could not care less about this whole subject," Lacey announces.

"Fine," I reply. "But be quiet, please. I'm trying to invent three things I like about you, and this is turning out to be a very hard assignment."

17

HIT ME WITH YOUR BEST SHOT!

AFTER A FEW MINUTES, LACEY GRABS HER
piece of notebook paper and writes on it for about
thirty seconds, tops. She signs her name at the
bottom of the page with a flourish.

And I'm still trying to think up one thing I like
about Lacey.

"That was fast," I say.

I am dying to see what she wrote, but I will not
give her the satisfaction of asking.

Lacey laughs. "I know the kind of stuff they want
to see," she tells me. "Just make something up."

"I was planning to," I mutter.

"Let's try it," Lacey says a few minutes later. She doesn't look at me when she says this, though. Instead, she examines her newly polished fingernails.

"Try what?"

"The good kind of fighting," Lacey says. "You know, compost fighting."

Is she serious? It must be a trick! She probably just wants to say more bad things about Susanna and Nibby.

"Poor little Ivy," Lacey teases—but more gently than usual. "Go ahead, tell me off. Hit me with your best shot! I can take it."

My heart starts beating a little faster. "OK," I say. "Well, it really hurt my feelings when you told me you hated it when I was born."

Lacey almost starts laughing. "Jeez, Ivy, I was only four years old at the time! It was nothing personal. I didn't even know you then."

"But you weren't four years old when you said it, were you?"

Lacey doesn't answer. And it is a very important question.

"Anyway," I conclude after a few moments, "I'm just telling you that it bothered me."

"OK. Sorry," Lacey says.

"Sorry for what? For feeling that way, or for saying it?" I ask.

"For saying it. Because I am not going to apolo-gize for the way I felt when I was four. I can't change the past."

"Well, but that's another thing," I tell her, talking faster now. "You keep saying that everything was better before I was born, but I can't change *that!*"

Now Lacey is examining her toenail polish. "Yeah, I guess not," she mumbles.

"And anyway," I continue, "things probably would have gotten worse in our family even without me. I can't take all the credit," I joke.

"I guess not," she says again.

Hey, I think I see her smiling a little.

"Anything else?" Lacey asks after a quiet minute or two.

"Well," I say, feeling a little stupid, "I'm still kind of mad at you about the scrapbook."

"The what?"

"Our scrapbook! You know, the one with all the pictures of cute little you in it and hardly any of me?"

"Oh, that scrapbook," Lacey says, laughing. "The one I never had anything to do with, or took any of the pictures for, right?"

"Ri-i-i-ight," I say reluctantly.

"Well, I'll make a deal with you, kid," Lacey says, slapping her knee like an auctioneer in an old-time Disney movie. "If you forgive me about not being in the scrapbook, I'll forgive you for wrecking the family when you were born. Deal?"

And I have to laugh, because it all sounds so dumb. "Deal," I say, and we shake hands.

I'm still a little suspicious, though. I can't help it.

18

A FEW SACRIFICES

"**O**OH, I FEEL ALL WARM AND TINGLY INSIDE,"
Lacey says, turning away. I guess she's suspicious
about our crazy agreement, too. "But shaking hands
doesn't exactly take care of *my* problem, does it?"

"What problem?"

"You know." She sighs and stretches. "The baby-
sitting thing. I know I'm probably going to have to
move back here with you and Mrs. Miller after
summer school ends. Mr. Miller's been really stressed
about how much room my stuff takes up in his apartment. And I hardly brought anything with me!"

I picture all the stacks of CDs she toted over there,
and the clothes, the makeup, the magazines and

paperbacks and hand-held video games and running shoes and shampoo bottles and . . .

"It's not as if that situation is going to improve," Lacey is saying, "what with Mrs. Miller taking classes now, and everything. And then what if she actually gets a job?"

"Well, first of all, it's not like I'm always going to be eleven," I point out. "And second, we can lie to her! Just leave me home alone," I suggest. "I won't tell anyone." *Let's just get this over with,* I am thinking.

But . . . alone at home. My hands turn cold even thinking about it, and I wipe them on my shorts.

Well, maybe I can pitch a tent in the backyard, or something.

Lacey tilts her head. "Wow, that's pretty gutsy of you, considering . . ." she says, but there's a hopeful look in her eyes.

Then she clouds up again and flops down on her half of the bed with a thud, right where the potato used to be. "It would never work," she says gloomily. "I'd be too worried about you to enjoy myself. See? Even when you're not with me, you're like this anchor I have to drag around wherever I go. And it drives me crazy to think maybe that's never, ever going to change."

She worries about me? I didn't know that. I can feel myself blushing.

Lacey continues to speak. "Mom and Dad always told me, 'Take care of your little sister. We're counting on you!' And I guess I just got so used to it that I can't break the habit."

"Well, break it," I snap. "I never asked you to worry about me."

"Yeah, you did. Kind of," Lacey says, shooting me a sideways look. "Whenever I talk to you, it's always 'poor little me.' Someone hurt your feelings at school. Nibby scratched you. Susanna's on vacation and you're bored. You have a headache."

I cannot believe what I am hearing! I can feel the hot tears coming, but I blink them back, because the last thing I want to do right now is cry in front of Lacey—and prove her right. Even if she *is* right! Because some of what she's said is true, I admit to myself. I have wanted her to take care of me, even to feel sorry for me, at times.

A few silent moments go by. "But won't you be scared, staying here alone?" Lacey finally asks softly.

I shake my head solemnly. "No," I lie.

Because if she worries about me, that must mean she loves me. And if she loves me, then I don't want her to worry about me anymore.

"Maybe I can go over to Susanna's house one afternoon a week," I tell Lacey, coming up with the idea on the spot. "I'll help Mrs. Reid in the garden, if necessary," I add, sounding brave—although secretly, as I've said before, I kind of like working in the Reids' garden. It's very relaxing. Compared to being at home, anyway.

"That would just be one day a week, though," she says gloomily.

"I'm not finished yet," I tell Lacey. "I can spend two afternoons at the library, even though I'd rather just come home and play with Nibby. That would give you three whole afternoons a week to trap yourself a boyfriend! And I won't tell Mr. and Mrs. Miller a thing."

Lacey giggles. "Well, it's not total freedom, but it would be better than nothing," she admits.

"Maybe you and I don't really have to get a sister divorce," I say a few minutes later. "We just have to untangle—like when you're dividing a plant."

Lacey groans. "Oh, no. Not another one of your weird theories," she says, rolling her eyes and clapping her hands over her ears.

I give her my funniest superior look. "If you don't want to hear about it, then I don't want to tell you."

"Oh, go ahead," she says. "There isn't anything else to do."

And so I tell her what Mrs. Reid taught me about dividing a plant to keep it healthy.

After I'm finished, Lacey clears her throat and says, "OK. One, it's nothing against your precious Susanna, but I think the Reids are kind of a bad influence on you, Ivy. And two, we aren't plants. Even if you are named after one."

"Yeah, but the situation is kind of the same," I point out.

Lacey just sighs again. "Why are you being so nice to me?" she finally asks.

And that is a very important question, too.

I could tell her that I want to make it up to her, about all the baby-sitting. Or that I love her, in spite of everything, or that I'm tired of all the fighting and just want to get out of this room. But I don't say any of that, because I do not feel like explaining these things. Even though all of them are true.

There is only so much you can—or should—say out loud. I've learned that much.

So I just shrug.

"And exactly what do I have to do for you in exchange for all these favors?" Lacey persists, sitting up suddenly from where she laid sprawled for the last few minutes. She looks alert, as if she is about to start taking notes. She also looks a little suspicious.

I can't think—fast, anyway—of anything she might do for me. "Stop teasing me so much?" I finally answer.

Lacey's eyes narrow, which is a sure sign that she is thinking.

"I could maybe fix your hair," she finally says.

"Huh?"

"I could fix your hair!"

"Yeah, I'll bet," I say, trying to smooth down my bangs. Which is hopeless. *Boi-i-i-ing!*

"Really, I mean it," Lacey says. "There's all kinds of mousse and stuff in Mrs. Miller's bathroom. And little scissors."

Scissors? She thinks I'd let her near me with scissors? After the knock-down, drag-out fight we had last night? "You'll just try to make me look even worse," I say.

"Ivy, you couldn't look any worse," Lacey tells me, and we both laugh—because she's right.

"OK, I'll let you comb my hair," I finally say. "But no cutting."

19

THE IVY CUT

WE LOOK AT EACH OTHER IN THE BATHROOM
mirror. My hair is wet, because I just washed it with
Lacey's shampoo—which doesn't smell so bad now.
She tries parting my hair in the middle, and I look
like I just escaped from *Little House on the Prairie.*

"What's it like being pretty?" I ask her.

"I'm not pretty," she says automatically.

People often say something like that when you
give them a compliment, I have noticed. I think it's
because they're not sure about it, and they want you
to go on and on, trying to convince them. Or they
are sure, and they just want to hear the compliment
one more time.

"Yes you are, and you know it," I tell her. "In fact, it's the only thing I wrote down so far on my list."

Lacey actually looks angry. "That I'm pretty?"

"What's wrong with that?" I ask, confused.

"Because—because that's just the way I was born," she sputters. "You should like a person because of the way they are, not because of the way they look."

Huh. I wouldn't mind if people liked me because they thought I was so amazingly beautiful that they couldn't even stand it, but I guess I see her point.

"Well, what did you write about me?" I ask, not even looking at Lacey in the mirror now. Instead, I stare down at the faucets—which could use a good cleaning, if you ask me.

Lacey jerks Mrs. Miller's comb back through the last snarls in my wet hair with a series of yanks that make my teeth clack together. "I said that you were funny," clack, "and that you're a good pet owner," clack, "and that you're a very–logical–person."

Clack, clack, clack.

"Thank you. Ow," I say, reaching up to rub the back of my head.

"You're welcome. And leave your hair alone— don't mess it up," Lacey snaps.

"Mess what up? It's not like I look any better!" I say, squinting my eyes in an attempt to make my whisk-broom bangs go away.

Lacey tosses down the comb. "I give up. I'm not a magician," she says. "Even I can't do anything with your hair—not the way it is."

I take a deep, shaky breath. "Then cut it off," I say.

Suspicious, she looks at me in the mirror. "Do you mean it?" she asks. I nod my head. "I really am pretty good at cutting hair, you know," she says, almost to herself.

"I know."

"But aren't you nervous?" Lacey-in-the-mirror asks me.

"I've been nervous my whole life," Ivy-in-the-mirror says.

Lacey combs her fingers through my hair experimentally. "Me, too, now that you mention it. Or for the last few months, anyway. Hmmm," she muses. "We could go with kind of a retro-punk look."

"Retro-punk?" I squeak. I can't help it—I sound even more nervous now. "Couldn't you maybe try something a little more . . . a little more I'm-about-to-start-a-new-school-and-my-hair-looks-perfectly-normal look?"

"Not with those bangs. But don't worry," she tries to reassure me. "I wouldn't do anything to you that I wouldn't let you do to me."

I begin to get excited. "You mean you'll let me cut your hair if I don't like what you do to mine?" I ask.

Lacey takes a step back. "That's not exactly what I said," she tells me.

I grab hold of my hair as if guarding it from Lacey.

But then I think about it. *My hair.* I hated the way it looked even before I cut the bangs. I've always wanted a short haircut. "Can we call it something else?" I ask.

"Huh?"

"My haircut," I say. "Let's call it something other than retro-punk."

"All right!" Lacey exclaims, giving the scissors a couple experimental snips. "You are definitely getting gutsier. We'll call it . . . The Divorce Cut."

"How about The Ivy Cut?" I suggest—meekly for once.

"Whatever," Lacey says, already concentrating hard on my hair.

I close my eyes, waiting for her to start snipping.

"Quick," Lacey says. "Keep your eyes shut and name three things you like about me."

"OK. One, you stick up for yourself," I say, my voice quavering. "Two, you're a very good fighter. And three, you are extremely talented when it comes to cutting hair."

"Hmmph! Let's hope so," Lacey says, and my haircut begins.

It's been at least twenty minutes, and my eyes are still shut, but I've been thinking. Trying to get up my nerve. "Is there any way that we can ever be friends again?" I finally ask Lacey.

Lacey runs her comb through the few hairs left on the back of my neck—which feels incredibly bare, I have to say. "Friends-friends?" she finally asks.

"Yeah."

"Probably not," Lacey says with a sigh so tiny I can barely hear it. Except I do.

"Well, what about sister-friends?" I ask, as if I don't really care whether the answer is yes or no.

"I guess we could try for that." I can almost see her shrug, only my eyes are still closed. The snips are farther apart now, which must mean that this haircut is drawing to a close.

But it could also mean that the haircut is so hopeless, she can't figure out what could possibly save it.

"All right, you can open your eyes after I count to three," Lacey says. She sounds scared.

"Count to five," I beg.

"OK, five. One, two, three, four—"

"Four and a half—" I interrupt.

"Five!"

Everything looks very bright in my parents' bathroom when I open my eyes.

The sound of Mrs. Pincus's radio drifts in through a partly open window. A mockingbird is singing nearby. She's guarding her nest, probably. They do that around here, even at night. In the summer, anyway.

Lacey is watching me.

I look at myself in the mirror.

And I give myself a great big grin. I look OK!

My hair is short, all right, but it's sort of wispy-short, not omigosh-I'm-in-prison!-short.

"You could even wear a little barrette or something," Lacey says, pulling a tuft of soft brown hair back to demonstrate.

"Yeah." I finger a curl. "We should take a picture."

Lacey smiles at me in the mirror. "We could start our own scrapbook," she says.

And my breath catches in my throat. Our own scrapbook!

Lacey holds the scissors out as if offering them to me. "So, do you like it, or do you want to cut my hair now?"

I take the scissors, still warm from Lacey's fingers. "You'd let me?" I ask her.

We look at each other, and for a moment, I see Lacey as Lacey-the-person, not Lacey-the-sister. I think that she sees Ivy-the-person, too.

For just a moment.

Maybe we *could* be friends someday.

"You'd let me?" I ask again, my voice a whisper.

"Are you out of your mind?" she whispers back.

There is a knock on the bathroom door. "Are you girls all right in there?" a worried voice asks. "I've got ice cream bars for you!"

"It's Mrs. Miller," Lacey informs me quietly.

"About time," I say.

Lacey giggles. "She's going to faint when she sees your hair. She'll be in shock."

"That's all right—I learned CPR in school last spring," I say. "Also the Heimlich maneuver, in case she chokes while she's yelling at us."

"Girls?"

"We're fine in here," Lacey calls out.

The door opens—very, very slowly. Cautiously, you could say.

"Surprise!" Lacey and I say at the exact same time.

20
A START

IT'S TWO WEEKS LATER, AND NO, EVERYONE is not living happily ever after, as Susanna once put it. But things are OK.

Lacey is still at Mr. Miller's apartment for now, even though summer school is over. But that is seeming more all right to everyone. She only cut class once—which was good, for her.

I've stayed home alone three times already. Once I even managed to stick it out inside the house. Nothing bad happened, either, if you don't count me almost having a heart attack when the mail got shoved through the slot at 10:57 A.M.

I finally rearranged the furniture in our bedroom,

and Lacey didn't say a word about it. Well, she hasn't actually seen it, yet. But Susanna loves it!

The new school year is going to start pretty soon, so Lacey will probably move home at that point—back into the rearranged room. And then we'll probably fight again.

That's just the way it is.

By the way, Mom and Dad absolutely detest it when we call them Mr. and Mrs. Miller—which, of course, makes it even more fun!

Nibby got loose for two whole days. Susanna and I made some really cool "Missing Rabbit" posters, and then Mrs. Pincus found him. He was chewing on the ancient newspapers in her garage, and she was *mad.* She said Nibby was obviously a very hostile rabbit who needed to get his chakras aligned.

I am watching Nibby much more closely now, just in case Mr. Miller was right—about some Americans eating some rabbits, I mean. Not about Nibby's chakras.

Whatever chakras are.

And our brand-new scrapbook looks pretty good, although we have filled just two pages so far. There are four pictures of Lacey and only three of me.

But hey, it's a start.

Sally Warner

Then

Now

As the middle of three children, Sally Warner grew up knowing what it was like to be a big sister *and* a little sister. That experience came in handy when she created the characters of Ivy and Lacey in *Sister Split.* Sally has written several other children's books as well, including *How to Be a Real Person (In Just One Day)*, *Finding Hattie*, *Sort of Forever*, and the popular Lily series. She is also an artist whose drawings have been exhibited around the country. Sally and her husband live in Southern California with their miniature wirehaired dachshund, Rocky.